Christmas at the Morning Glory

Reva Davenport

Christmas at the Morning Glory
© 2025 by Reva Davenport

For information, please contact: **Reva Davenport**
info@revadavenport.com

Cover design by Reva Davenport

Published by: Marigold Lake Press

First Edition: 2025

For every small-town Christmas spirit—
the cocoa drinkers, the carol singers, the Bunco players,
and all those who know the magic of community,
laughter, and a little holiday mystery.

Contents

Welcome to Marigold Lake

Where every mystery comes with cocoa, cookies,
and a Boston Terrier named Sadie.
Small-town charm, quirky neighbors,
and a dash of holiday mischief await you
at the Morning Glory B&B.

Prologue

If Christmas in Marigold Lake had a soundtrack, it would be equal parts jingle bells and gossip.

From my spot on the Morning Glory's front porch, I could hear both: the church bells chiming down the block, and Barb Simmons loudly announcing to anyone within range that "this year's festival would either go down in history or go up in flames." With Barb, those two things were usually the same.

Sadie, my Boston Terrier, leaned against my shin, ears twitching like tiny antennae. She gave a short huff, which I interpreted as agreement—or maybe impatience. Boston Terriers are experts at both.

"Don't start," I told her, adjusting the garland around the porch railing. "We're already behind schedule."

She sneezed, unimpressed, and promptly sat on the end of the ribbon I was trying to tie.

The truth was that the whole town felt behind schedule. Decorations were still half up, the carolers sounded more like a warm-up act than a choir, and the giant evergreen in the square leaned ever so slightly to the left like it had overindulged in cocoa. Normally, Marigold Lake thrived on that brand of small-town chaos. But this year, there was a tension underneath the tinsel.

The missing star had been the first clue. Our beloved metal star—part heirloom, part beacon—had disappeared from the town hall attic. Some whispered Maple Valley stole it to sabotage our festival; others swore it was an inside job. Either way, Christmas didn't feel quite right without it.

Across the street, the Petersons were dragging out their inflatable reindeer while bickering at full volume. Mrs. Peterson wanted "tasteful." Mr. Peterson wanted "more lights than the Griswold's." Their compromise looked like Santa's sleigh crash-landed into a snowdrift of extension cords.

Sadie, apparently deciding the reindeer were enemies of the state, barked ferociously, then lunged forward—straight into the string of garland I'd just hung. Within seconds she was wrapped in pine and twinkle lights, strutting proudly like a four-legged parade float.

"Great," I muttered, untangling her. "Festive sabotage from my own dog."

The truth was, if you squinted, the whole town looked picture-perfect—snow frosting the rooftops, Main Street lined with candy-cane poles, the lake in the distance glimmering like a silver platter. But up close, there were cracks: the leaning tree, the missing star, the frayed nerves that no amount of cocoa could disguise.

"See?" I whispered to Sadie as I freed her from the last bit of ribbon. "Normal chaos. Nothing to worry about."

But even as I said it, a shiver crept under my scarf. Because if there was one thing I'd learned since moving back to Marigold Lake, it was this: Christmas here always came with complications.

And this year, the complications had already begun.

Sadie pawed at the door, ready to head inside. I followed, tugging my coat tighter, casting one last glance toward the crooked tree in the square.

Somewhere in the twinkle and tinsel, mischief was waiting. And I had the uneasy feeling we were about to stumble right into it.

Chapter One

Tinsel and Trouble

By eight a.m., the Morning Glory looked like a snow globe that had been shaken by an over-caffeinated elf... twice... then dropped, picked up, and shaken again for good measure.

Garland draped the banister in thick, festive loops, shedding the occasional glitter flake like it was molting. A wreath the size of a hula hoop hugged the front door with the enthusiasm of a relative who doesn't know when to let go. The parlor glowed with lamplight bouncing off polished wood floors, and the pine tree in the bay window wore gold twinkle lights like it knew it had won the seasonal beauty pageant.

The only un-festive element was me—standing at the bottom of the stairs with a box of tangled extension cords, staring into its depths as though trying to read tea leaves. Past-Claire, in a moment of misguided optimism, had labeled the cords "green," "other green," and "not that green." Present-Claire regretted every life choice that had led to this moment.

Sadie, my Boston Terrier and the Morning Glory's self-appointed Chief Executive of Everything, sat in the hallway wearing her red scarf and the unimpressed expression of someone evaluating my job performance.

"Don't judge me," I told her, shaking the cords in what was supposed to be a confident manner but ended up more like a sad rattle. "This is the price of Christmas magic."

She snorted—one of her signature unimpressed snorts—then circled like she was auditioning for a runway show. The look she gave me said: *Move along, human. The cocoa situation requires oversight.*

She was right. Something always required oversight at the Morning Glory during the holiday season.

Right on cue, the swinging kitchen door burst open and Hannah barreled into the hallway on a gust of cinnamon and sugar. Her cheeks were flushed, her blond bun precariously held together by a candy cane clip that had clearly seen combat.

"Claire!" she gasped, wide-eyed and breathless. "We have cocoa, we have gingerbread, we have people who treat gingerbread as a breakfast food—bless them—but we also have a minor spice situation."

"With you," I said, "minor covers everything from 'oops' to 'please call the fire department.' What kind?"

She winced. Never a good sign. "Let's call it... lively cocoa. I grabbed the wrong jar." She lowered her voice. "Cayenne."

I closed my eyes. "Ah. Spicy cheer."

"Already fixed it." She lifted a tray of sugar-dusted gingerbread men like a peace offering. "Finn drank the first pot without blinking. Said his sinuses have never been better."

"That explains why I can hear him singing 'Jingle Bell Rock' through two walls and a staircase."

As if summoned by the mention of his name, Finn's playlist let out a crackle from the living room speaker, followed by an overly enthusiastic guitar riff. Our resident handyman-slash-IT wizard had been here since dawn, rehanging icicle lights and attempting to sync the porch timer—a quest he waged every December like a knight with a vendetta.

Finn approached life with three tools: zip ties, firmware updates, and raw enthusiasm. It was anyone's guess which one would fix a problem and which would cause the toaster to flash Morse code again.

A knock rattled the front door. Before I could get there, Barb swept in, trailing December air and enough gossip to heat a church basement.

She wore a quilted coat with a faux-fur collar large enough to classify as wildlife. Her lipstick was a fierce Christmas red, aimed straight for my cheek as she swooped in.

"Morning, dear!" she declared, shedding her coat onto the newel post like the Morning Glory had been constructed specifically for her convenience. "Have you heard? Don't faint. No—do faint. I'll catch you."

"It's barely eight," I warned.

"Exactly when tragedies happen." She pressed a hand to her chest, eyes widening dramatically. "The star is gone."

Hannah froze. I froze. Sadie froze so completely she looked carved from festive marble.

"The *star*?" I echoed.

"Off the town tree," Barb whispered, scandal dripping from every syllable. "Gone—poof—somewhere between the lighting ceremony and dawn. People are pretending everything's fine, but I know the difference between calm and 'we're five minutes from forming a mob.'"

Hannah clutched her tray. "Not *the* star? The one that's been on top since—"

"Since the year our marching band won regionals," Barb said. "We all pretended it was basically the Rose Bowl. That star is history. That star is tradition. That star makes grown men cry."

I set the box of cords down with the care one uses for bomb disposal. Because this? This was a bomb.

The town star wasn't fancy. It was welded locally decades ago, repainted every few years, and hauled onto the tree by a rotating roster of firefighters with questionable judgment. But in Marigold Lake, nothing unified people quite like Christmas—and nothing symbolized Christmas more than that star.

"Maybe it was wind," Hannah offered, though her voice wavered.

"Wind doesn't undo hooks and vanish into the night," Barb said flatly. "Sheriff's office claims it might have 'fallen.'" She made aggressive air quotes that could have sliced fruit. "Meanwhile, I saw three Maple Valley cars on Main Street at dawn."

Ah, Maple Valley. Our rival. Our frenemy. Our constant thorn wrapped in tinsel.

Their cheer committee had matching jackets. Their cocoa had notes. Their carolers warmed up before performing.

"It could be a prank," I said, though something sharp and cold edged into my stomach. Losing the star didn't feel like mischief. It felt... intentional.

Barb leaned in until her glittery eyeshadow invaded personal space. "Mark my words, Claire Fisher. This is an attack."

"On Christmas?" I tried to joke.

"Exactly on Christmas," she said with triumphant solemnity.

Hannah shoved gingerbread men into both our hands. "We'll figure it out," she said. Whether she meant the star or the sudden spike in town anxiety was unclear.

"Want me to bring cocoa to the station?" she asked.

"Yes," I said. "And tell Matt it's regular cocoa again. No cayenne."

Barb bit the head off her cookie like she was carrying out a personal vendetta. "Speaking of Detective Hale—" She nodded toward the door. "Ask and ye shall receive."

The door swung open and Matt stepped inside, stamping snow from his boots. He wore a dark peacoat, a dusting of frost in his hair, and that expression he got whenever he arrived anywhere in Marigold Lake: cautious optimism tempered by the knowledge chaos lurked around every corner.

His eyes softened when he saw me. "Hey. You hear?"

"About the star?" I said. "We heard."

Sadie rushed forward, whole backside wagging. Matt crouched, scratched behind her ears, and whispered, "Hi, partner. Ready to solve a case? Or just supervise crumbs?"

She sneezed, which was as affirmative as it got.

Matt straightened, face sobering. "You okay?"

Barb didn't let me speak. "She's devastated. *I'm* devastated. Hannah is stress-baking. The town is in crisis."

"I stress-bake every day," Hannah said.

Matt's mouth twitched. "We're looking into it. Could be kids. Could be someone wanting a souvenir." His eyes flicked to me—*please do not climb the tree.*

"I wasn't going to climb the tree," I said automatically.

One eyebrow rose.

"Right now," I added.

He sighed with affection. "Claire... please don't climb the tree ever."

"Fine," I said.

His radio crackled softly. "I'm headed back to the square. Wanted to check on you."

"That's a very smooth way of saying 'please give me gingerbread,'" I said, handing him one.

He nibbled it like it was state-issued relief. "Thanks."

He glanced around the parlor. "Looks good."

"It'll look better when Finn convinces the porch lights to behave."

From the foyer, Finn called, "It's the timer! The timer is a liar!"

Matt gave me an apologetic look. "I'll circle back later."

"You know where to find me," I said.

He reached the door, then paused. "Claire?"

"Hm?"

"Don't go investigating without me."

Barb clucked. "She won't. *We* will."

Matt closed his eyes in the expression of a man reconsidering his life choices. "I'm leaving before I say something I can't take back." He saluted Sadie and disappeared into the cold.

When the door shut, Hannah gave me a side glance. "So. We're not investigating... without him."

"We're absolutely not," I said. "We're just... noticing."

"Noticing," she repeated reverently.

By nine a.m., the Morning Glory had settled into its usual breakfast hum—the kind of low, contented murmur that always reminded me of a teapot just beginning to whistle. Guests chatted over pancakes, the radiator hissed like it was offering commentary, and outside the windows, snow fell in lazy flakes that made the porch rail look dipped in powdered sugar.

I floated between tables with a coffeepot in one hand and Sadie in my wake, doing her usual patrol for dropped bacon. The air smelled like pine, gingerbread scones, and the cocoa Hannah was determined to perfect before the weekend crowds descended.

At the corner table, the Palmers—the retired teacher couple—sat in matching cable-knit sweaters that appeared to have been purchased as a set, possibly in 1997.

"Is it true?" Mrs. Palmer whispered the moment I approached. Her voice held the conspiratorial intensity of someone delivering state secrets. "About the star?"

I opened my mouth to deliver my carefully crafted, non-panic-inducing response, but Mr. Palmer leaned forward and murmured, "Maple Valley," like he was uttering a password.

"We're keeping an open mind," I said, adopting the calm tone I reserved for public-relations emergencies and malfunctioning waffle irons. "There's no evidence yet."

"There will be," Mrs. Palmer said confidently. "Trouble never comes alone. In all my years of teaching, the moment one child threw a snowball, a second child was drafting a battle strategy."

Sadie snorted approvingly.

Across the room, the anniversary couple—Darla and Ron—were cutting their pancakes into mirror-image triangles. They'd barely spoken since checking in yesterday. I had a suspicion that the Morning Glory holiday atmosphere had either rekindled something... or pushed something to the brink.

Meanwhile, the father/daughter duo at the far table was deep into a discussion about campus tours and majors, though the daughter kept sneaking glances out the window at the slowly gathering snow. It struck me then how many pieces of life passed through this house—celebrations, worries, transitions, secrets. Maybe that made people more observant. Or more nervous. Or both.

I cleared dishes, refilled mugs, offered Hannah's fresh gingerbread scones, and tried not to think about the star sitting somewhere in the cold, cut from the tree like someone had snipped the top off a holiday postcard.

The kitchen door swung open behind me, and Hannah slipped out with her oven mitts still on.

"You think it was kids?" she whispered, lowering her voice so only I could hear. "I mean—stealing the star is stupid, but it's also daring. High-risk, high-idiocy."

"It's ten feet tall," I said. "If kids took it, they're either working in teams or training for Santa's Strongman Competition."

"Ugh." She made a face. "Now I'm picturing a teenager bench-pressing ornaments."

Before I could respond, Finn poked his head in, expression a combination of triumph and static electricity. "Timer fixed! I wooed it with logic. And threats." He held out an envelope. "Also, someone left this on the front desk for you."

My name was written on the front in plain block letters. No stickers. No mistletoe doodles. Just... clinical.

My stomach tightened.

I opened it carefully.

Inside was a printed flyer for Maple Valley's *Hometown Holiday Bash*—their big cross-town rival event. And at the bottom, scrawled in black marker:

Merry X-Mess.

A hollow elevator-drop feeling settled behind my ribs.

"Where did you find this?" I asked quietly.

"Right on the bell," Finn said. "No one in the foyer. I checked the porch cam—we'll look at that next."

Right on cue—like she had been summoned by the scent of drama—Barb materialized behind us.

"What did I tell you?" she exclaimed, stabbing a perfectly manicured finger at the scribbled message. "This has Maple Valley written all over it. And probably bought with a coupon."

"Or," Hannah said carefully, "maybe someone wants us to think it's Maple Valley."

"That's what I'm afraid of," I murmured.

Before we could dissect it further, a crash in the dining room made all three of us jump. Sadie bolted ahead like she'd been shot out of a festive cannon.

We found Mr. Palmer apologizing while a toppled sugar caddy spilled packets like confetti across the table.

"Terribly sorry," he said. "My elbow has a mind of its own."

"It's all right," I said, sweeping up rogue sugar and ignoring the unpleasant thrum in my chest.

The flyer was still in my hand, its ink stark and too bold.

Someone wanted attention. Maybe a laugh. Maybe chaos.

Either way, I didn't like it.

Back at the front desk, I slid the flyer into a folder labeled EVENT INCIDENTS, which I'd once used for loose paperwork but suspected would soon become the unofficial evidence log of the apocalypse.

The bell dinged.

I looked up nervously—not sure I was ready for another surprise—and saw a young woman bundled in a holly-berry-red puffer coat. Snow dusted her curls; her cheeks were rosy from the cold.

"Hi," she said brightly. "Any chance you have two rooms available? We were headed for Maple Valley, but they said their lights are... delayed," she added tactfully. "And your place looks like a postcard."

"We do," I said, smile shifting into place out of habit. "Welcome to the Morning Glory. I'm Claire."

"I'm Becca." She gestured behind her. "This is my aunt, Linda."

Aunt Linda stepped inside with the purposeful efficiency of someone trained in disaster preparedness. Sensible boots. Sensible coat. Eyes that scanned the foyer like she was checking exits.

"Do you lock your doors at night?" she asked immediately.

"Um... yes," I said.

"Good. People make foolish decisions at Christmas."

Her tone wasn't suspicious. Just... factual. Which was somehow even more unsettling.

Becca nudged her. "She listens to too many true-crime podcasts."

"Better to listen than star in one," Aunt Linda replied.

I processed their check-in, gave them the morning schedule, and watched with interest as Aunt Linda paused at the bay-window tree. Her gaze softened—just a fraction—before reassembling into brisk preparedness.

When they went upstairs, I exhaled.

Sadie was staring at me, head cocked. She always knew when something felt off. And Aunt Linda, with her strange blend of warmth and suspicion, hadn't set off a red flag... but maybe a pink one.

"Okay," I said, returning to the kitchen. "We get through the last few checkouts, then—"

"—we go 'noticing,'" Barb said, having already claimed a wingback chair like a general establishing headquarters.

"Yes," I said. "Carefully. Respectfully. With hats."

Finn reappeared, cheeks pink from cold. "By the way," he said. "I checked the porch cam. Someone was on our walkway at 12:23 a.m."

Game-changer.

The room fell silent.

"Describe," I said.

"Tall. Hooded. Didn't come up the steps. Just... stood. Then walked toward Main Street."

A thin ribbon of cold snaked down my spine.

"Could be a late-night stroller," Hannah said, always the optimist.

"Or a porch-prowling menace," Barb said, because she never met a crisis she didn't adopt.

I looked at the folder containing the flyer. At the empty spot on the town tree ten blocks away. At Sadie, leaning warm against my leg like she was trying to anchor me.

"Okay," I said slowly. "We'll pass it to Matt. And we'll—"

"—wear hats," Barb finished.

"—and lock our doors," I added, thinking of Aunt Linda's very pointed question.

Outside, snow drifted heavier—quiet, relentless, settling over the town like a blanket pulling tight.

The Morning Glory glowed against it, warm and inviting.

Too inviting.

"Claire?" Hannah asked softly. "You think whoever took the star will stop there?"

I looked at the lights on the banister. The wreath. The tree. The flyer.

The hookless empty top of the town tree—ripped clean.

"No," I said.

And the truth of it settled deep and cold.

"I don't."

By midmorning, the snowfall had shifted from gentle postcard flakes to a determined curtain that swept across the street in shimmering white. The Morning Glory's porch light haloed each flake, making the whole front walk look like a stage just waiting for some dramatic entrance.

Unfortunately, drama in Marigold Lake rarely waited for an invitation.

Hannah, who was now on her fourth batch of gingerbread scones, slid a warm one toward me on a plate. "Eat," she said. "Before your blood sugar drops and you start accusing our elderly guests of grand theft star."

"I'm not accusing anyone," I said.

Yet.

Sadie hopped onto the stool beside me, her expression making it clear she would like to assist with any interrogation involving baked goods.

The kitchen door swung open with Finn's usual burst of chaotic energy, static still clinging to his hair like he'd been headbutting tinsel garland.

"Okay," he said, grabbing a mug. "I've synced the porch cam with the cloud, backed up the backup, and installed an anti-snooping protocol."

"Which means?" I asked.

"It means if someone tries to tamper with our footage now, the camera will scream," he said proudly.

Hannah blinked. "Scream?"

He grinned. "Digitally."

"So like... beep?"

"No, like... scream."

I pinched the bridge of my nose. "Finn, please don't unintentionally traumatize holiday tourists."

He held up three fingers. "Scout's honor. The screaming is only if tampering occurs. Or maybe weather interference. Or..." His voice trailed off as he saw my expression. "It's fine. It'll be fine."

Before I could question that further, Barb bustled in, cheeks flushed with the thrill of collecting new intel.

"Ladies, gentlemen, and small hero dog," she began, nodding respectfully at Sadie, "I have news."

"We're listening," I said, bracing myself.

She leaned over the counter, lowering her voice. "While I was walking past the square just now, I overheard Doris Temple telling her sister that she saw footprints at the base of the tree."

"That seems... expected," Hannah said. "People were at the lighting last night."

"These footprints," Barb said dramatically, "were *fresh*."

Finn frowned. "Fresh as in... recent?"

"Fresh as in," Barb whispered, "this morning."

That got my attention.

"Size?" I asked. "Direction? Boot vs. shoe?"

Barb rolled her eyes. "Sweetheart, if I'd measured them, I'd be drafting a report right now. All I know is Doris said they were deep. Heavy. Like someone carrying something."

My stomach tightened. "Carrying the star?"

"Or dragging it," Barb said grimly. "Depending on upper-body strength."

Sadie barked sharply, jumping down and charging to the foyer window. She stood on her hind legs, front paws on the sill, ears perked, body rigid.

I followed her gaze.

A figure moved along the sidewalk across the street—hood up, shoulders hunched against the snow. Not unusual for winter. What *was* unusual was the way the person paused directly across from the Morning Glory.

Just stood.

Like they were looking.

Or checking.

Or waiting.

A flicker of something electric crawled up my spine.

"Do you see that?" I whispered.

Finn joined me at the window, squinting. "Hmm. Hooded. Tall-ish. Hard to tell much else."

"Could be nothing," Hannah said from behind me, though her tone carried the brittle edge of someone trying to believe their own optimism.

The figure shifted, took one slow step backward—

—and disappeared into the veil of falling snow.

Gone.

Finn reached for the porch-cam app on his phone. "Got it."

Sadie growled low, her little body vibrating like a coffee mug on a wobbly table.

I exhaled, pressing a hand to my chest.

"Okay," I said. "We're going to take this seriously. We'll watch the footage, we'll stay alert, and we'll get Matt's team involved before this turns into a full town panic spiral."

"Oh, honey," Barb said, patting my shoulder sympathetically, "the panic spiral started at 8:04 this morning. You're just catching up."

Before I could respond, the front door opened, bringing in a swirl of snow—and the scent of cinnamon from the street vendor cart outside.

Aunt Linda stepped back inside, tracking snowflakes in a perfect line behind her. She stopped short when she saw all of us staring at the window like we expected the Ghost of Christmas Chaos to appear.

She raised a brow. "Everything all right?"

"Just... weather," I said quickly. "And... holiday enthusiasm."

"Hmm." She assessed the tension in the air, the way Sadie was still bristling, the tightness around Hannah's smile. "Well," she said briskly, "remember what I said. People do foolish things at Christmas."

Then she walked upstairs, snow melting in tiny droplets along her path.

After a long moment, Finn exhaled. "I don't like this."

"Me neither," I said.

Hannah rubbed her arms. "It's starting to feel deliberate."

Behind us, Barb crossed her arms with firm conviction. "Ladies, I'm telling you—this isn't about kids or pranks or festive mischief. We are dealing with something organized. Calculated. Maybe even—" she leaned in dramatically "—a Christmas conspiracy."

Normally I would've laughed. Today, the word didn't feel so funny.

I straightened, smoothing the front of my sweater. "All right. We'll loop Matt in, finish breakfast service, then start checking with people around Main Street. Someone saw something. Someone heard something."

"And we'll wear hats," Barb added solemnly.

"Lots of hats," Finn agreed.

Hannah handed me another scone and squeezed my hand. "We've got this. We always do."

Sadie nudged my leg, staring up at me with that steady, brave look of hers.

I smiled down at her. "Right, partner?"

She gave a single, confident *woof*.

Outside, the snow kept falling. The lights on the banister twinkled. The Morning Glory stood warm and bright against the cold.

Somewhere in town, someone had stolen our star.
Someone had left a message.
Someone had hovered on our walkway in the dark.

And someone had just watched the B&B from across the street.

I didn't know who—or what they wanted—
but a quiet certainty settled inside me like a new ornament placed carefully on a tree:

This wasn't over.
Not even close.

And Christmas in Marigold Lake was about to get a whole lot more complicated.

Chapter Two

Market Day Mayhem

Saturday mornings in Marigold Lake always meant the winter market—a cheerful tangle of produce stalls, craft booths, and enough gossip to power the streetlamps. Normally, I loved it. Today, after the star debacle, it felt like a crime scene with cinnamon rolls.

Snow dusted the sidewalks in a thin, sparkling layer, the kind that squeaked under boots. Vendors had lined Main Street with pop-up tents and tables, all strung with twinkle lights and pine garland. A brass quartet near the gazebo was butchering "Deck the Halls" with gusto, and the air smelled like kettle corn, wood smoke, and the faint metallic tang of collective anxiety.

"Eyes open," Barb said, marching at my side with her scarf flapping like a cape in the wind. She'd upgraded from her usual knit hat to a red beret with a rhinestone snowflake that glared at passersby. "Saboteurs always circle back to admire their handiwork."

"They also sell kettle corn," Hannah pointed out, trying to keep pace while balancing Sadie's leash in one hand and a bag of cranberries in the other. "Can we circle back to that instead?"

Sadie trotted ahead, nose to the ground, nub tail twitching like a radar. Every few steps she gave a sharp sniff at a booth, then sneezed dramatically, as if uncovering evidence no one else could see. Her breath puffed in little clouds, and she kept shooting me looks that said, plainly, If you would just let me run this operation, we'd be done by now.

We passed Mrs. Kline's jam table, where jars of ruby-red strawberry and deep purple blackberry were lined in soldiers' rows, each lid topped with a crimson gingham square.

"Morning, Claire," Mrs. Kline called, voice warm. Then, in a lower whisper: "You hear about the star?"

"We heard," I said, because apparently that was my new line.

She clucked her tongue. "It's a sign, that's what it is. Ever since they put those LED bulbs in the streetlamps, nothing's been right. Too cold. Angels don't like LED."

Barb scribbled that down.

"Please don't write 'angels vs. LED' in your notes," I murmured.

"Too late," she said, not looking up. "It's under 'possible spiritual sabotage.'"

We moved on.

At the next stall, a young couple from out of town sold handmade candles in little mason jars. Labels read things like Cabin at Midnight and Grandma's Kitchen. I picked one up and sniffed. Cinnamon, vanilla, and... what was that? Regret?

"Holiday Overcommitment," the woman explained shyly. "Cinnamon, coffee, and a little pine-smoke. I thought it captured the season."

"Too real," Hannah said, but she bought one anyway.

Sadie snuffled under the table and emerged with a pinecone stuck to her chin. The candle-seller laughed, but her gaze flicked nervously toward the square, where the town tree towered—temporarily starless.

"It looks so wrong without it," she said softly.

I followed her gaze. Even from here, the empty hook on top felt like a missing tooth in a familiar smile.

"Look at that," Barb hissed suddenly, pointing at a display of popcorn garlands two stalls down. "Three strands missing from the end. Classic supply sabotage."

"Or classic hungry squirrels," I said.

"Don't downplay this, Claire. Squirrels are agents of chaos."

"To be fair," Hannah added, "they did attack Doris's scarecrow last fall."

"That was a coordinated strike," Barb said.

Before I could argue, Doris Temple popped up from behind a table of crocheted mittens like a festive meerkat. Her binoculars dangled from her neck, clacking against a knit sweater covered in UFOs wearing Santa hats.

"I heard the star was stolen by professional thieves," she whispered, eyes wide. "Like in those Hallmark heist movies."

"Pretty sure those aren't a genre," I said.

"They should be," she retorted. "Alien thieves. In trench coats. With tasteful scarves."

"Aliens again?" Hannah groaned.

"Aliens then," Doris declared. "Christmas lights draw them."

Hannah pressed a mitten to her forehead. "I need cocoa."

We wove through the stalls, pausing to greet neighbors and endure whispers. Everywhere we went, someone had a theory.

"It's Maple Valley," muttered Mr. Holloway from behind a pyramid of apples so perfect they looked fake. He adjusted his John Deere cap and leaned in. "Their cheer committee's been smug for years. Smug people steal stars."

"Teenagers," Mrs. Miller insisted, clutching a bag of carrots with the intensity of a woman holding evidence. "If you ask me, kids have too much time and not enough responsibility. And you know how strong they get from all that sports. They can lift things."

"Government cover-up," Doris chimed in again, because she apparently had a rotating list.

Barb scribbled furiously in her notebook, nodding as if each theory was gospel. "All suspects. No one is above suspicion. Not even the carrot woman."

Sadie chose that moment to hop up against Mrs. Miller's apron, leaving a dusty paw print across her carrots.

"See?" Mrs. Miller said, triumphant. "The dog knows."

"I'm so sorry," I said, dragging Sadie back, cheeks hot.

Sadie licked a stray carrot, then spat it out like it had personally offended her.

"See?" Hannah said. "Sadie has standards."

We passed a stall where hand-carved birdhouses hung from a wooden rack. Old Mr. Weatherby sat on a folding chair behind the table, bundled in so many layers he looked like a cranky marshmallow.

"Morning, Claire," he said. "Tell your handyman I'm still waiting on him to look at my porch railing."

"I'll remind Finn," I said. "Busy week."

Weatherby sniffed. "Busy losing our star to Maple Valley, you mean." His eyes narrowed. "You mark my words. Those people have always wanted what we've got."

"What's that?" I asked lightly. "Our charming municipal potholes?"

He ignored me. "First it's the star. Next thing, it'll be the whole festival."

The wind picked up, carrying a stray page from a flyer down the street. It skittered across the snow like a startled bird and plastered itself against my boot. I reached down and peeled it off: Maple Valley's Hometown Holiday Bash. A tear down the side had cut through the word Bash, leaving BA in bold red.

Merry X-Mess, the scrawl from the flyer at the B&B flashed in my mind.

I folded the paper and tucked it into my pocket.

"Claire!" Hannah tugged my sleeve. "Please tell me we're getting cocoa now. My hands have lost feeling."

"Cocoa," I agreed. "Even sleuths need sugar."

We steered toward the cocoa stand, where a local church youth group had set up an operation so efficient it could've handled airport traffic. Three kids poured, two took money, and one sprinkled marshmallows with the solemnity of a priest.

"That's my kind of religion," Hannah said reverently.

We each took a steaming cup. Mine smelled reassuringly like chocolate and not at all like cayenne.

"Can you believe this?" murmured a voice behind me.

I turned to see Grace Holloway, clutching a to-go cup, eyes shadowed. Her gift shop was just visible at the end of the street, its window display crowded with ceramic snowmen and painted ornaments.

"About the star?" I asked.

"And the rumors," she said. "People talking like Hometown Christmas is cursed. I've had three cancellations this morning alone. 'We'll wait and see how things shake out,' they say." Her mouth twisted. "You can't sell hope on lay-away."

My heart tugged. "We're going to fix it," I said. "Find the star. Stop whoever's doing this. People will come."

"Better," Barb murmured to herself, "'Christmas Sabotage: The Curse of the Missing Star.' I'll workshop it."

Grace's gaze flitted to Barb's notebook, then back to the square. "Just... be careful who you accuse. People get mean when they're scared."

She drifted away, shoulders hunched against the cold.

Hannah watched her go, frowning. "She's been on edge since that new gift shop opened in Maple Valley, the one with all the imported ornaments."

"Right," I said. "The one with the hand-blown glass angels we definitely can't afford."

"Those," Hannah confirmed. "Can't blame her for resenting Maple Valley, honestly."

Another red thread tugged itself through my mental board: Grace's struggling shop, Maple Valley's shinier competition, a missing town centerpiece that could push tourists next door.

I sipped my cocoa and pretended my stomach wasn't tightening.

That's when I spotted Matt.

He stood near the bakery tent, coat open against the cold, talking quietly with one of the stall owners. His posture was relaxed, but his eyes swept the crowd like he was cataloging every suspicious snow boot in town. Even from here, I could see the little crease between his brows—the one that only showed up when he was worrying about more than he let on.

Barb gasped and elbowed me so hard I sloshed cocoa onto my glove. "Undercover detective work! Look at him blend."

"He's literally six feet tall in a town of flannel," I said, licking chocolate from my knuckles. "Blending isn't his gift."

"Disagree," Barb said. "He looks like any other ruggedly handsome Christmas movie love interest."

"Stop narrating my life like you're holding a remote," I muttered.

Matt caught my eye, and something like relief flickered across his face. He excused himself from the stall owner and joined us, giving Sadie a scratch behind the ears. She practically melted, traitorous little ham.

"Morning," he said. His tone was calm, but I caught the tightness at the edge of it. "Hear anything useful?"

"Everything," Barb declared. "Aliens. Squirrels. Teenagers with bodybuilder strength. Doris is convinced it's intergalactic."

"It's not not intergalactic," Doris called from three stalls away, because apparently her hearing was bionic.

Matt gave me a look over Barb's head, the kind that said help me.

"Mostly gossip," I translated. "But people are spooked. Everyone's pointing fingers."

He nodded. "Figured. We're checking the square for footprints, but snow covered most of them overnight. The camera on the corner flickered around midnight; we're pulling what we can. If you notice anything out of place..." His gaze lingered on me. "...tell me before Barb organizes a sting operation."

"Too late," Barb said. "I'm drafting one tonight. Working title: Starfall. Subtitle: A Town Betrayed."

Matt pinched the bridge of his nose and muttered something about Florida.

"Any real leads?" I asked.

He hesitated, which I did not like. "We've got a few possibilities. Firefighters who had access to the ladder truck. Kids who hang around the square late. A couple of Maple Valley plates spotted on Main after midnight."

"How do you know that?" Hannah asked.

He tapped his temple. "Old Mrs. Jenkins sleeps in her recliner by the front window and narrates the street like a police scanner. She called dispatch at 12:17 a.m. to report a suspicious sedan turning around twice."

"Bless her," Barb said. "Living security camera."

"Living security camera with cataracts," Matt amended. "But still. We can't ignore it."

His radio crackled and a voice murmured something I couldn't make out. His jaw tensed.

"I've gotta circle back," he said. "Chief wants an update before the noon rush."

"Tell Chief Cowell I said hi," Barb chirped. "And that if he needs civilian consultants, my calendar is wide open."

Matt pretended not to hear her. "Seriously," he told me, voice low. "If you see anything—call. Don't go investigating without backup."

"Of course," I said, nodding solemnly.

He narrowed his eyes. "Claire..."

"We're just noticing," I said. "Noticing is practically a civic duty."

"Noticing is step one to 'I can explain, officer,'" he said.

Hannah snorted into her cocoa.

Matt sighed, but there was affection in it. "You're exhausting."

"And yet, here you are," I said.

He gave me a look that was half exasperation, half something softer, then turned and strode back into the crowd.

Hannah watched him go, then sighed into her cocoa. "You two are exhausting to watch."

I ignored her and focused on Sadie, who had wedged herself under a table of scented candles and emerged with a cinnamon votive stuck to her collar. The vendor laughed nervously as I pried it loose.

"Sorry," I said. "She's running her own side investigation."

Barb clapped her hands. "See? Even the dog is gathering evidence."

"Or free samples," I muttered, but I pocketed the little candle anyway. Cinnamon, with a hint of smoke. Another smell to associate with this morning's unease.

We made another pass down the block, ostensibly to look at handmade scarves but really to listen. A man in a Maple Valley ski cap argued loudly with a woman over booth space. A teenage boy in a hoodie lurked near the edges, face half-hidden, fingers drumming on the back of a bench. An older woman complained to anyone who would listen that "this never would have happened when Mayor Pritchard was in office," as if former elected officials were talismans against petty crime.

"Hey, did you hear?" someone near the kettle corn stand murmured. "My cousin says there's a guy staying in Maple Valley asking questions about our festival. Says he's 're-searching small-town dynamics.' Sounds shady if you ask me."

My head turned before I could stop it. I caught only a glimpse of the speaker—a woman in a purple parka—and the man she spoke to, who shrugged and said, "Probably a blogger," but the words lodged in my brain.

Someone asking questions. Someone watching both towns.

A snowflake landed on my eyelashes. I blinked it away.

By the time we left the market, our bags were full of cranberries, cookies, a candle, and at least two new suspects. The whispers about Maple Valley had spread but so had the tension. Every sideways glance felt like another string pulled loose.

Sadie trotted ahead toward the B&B, paws leaving neat little prints in the snow. Hannah trudged beside me, clutching her cocoa like a talisman.

"This is supposed to be my favorite weekend," she said quietly. "Christmas market, baking marathon, too many people asking if I can cater their office parties..."

"You can still have all that," I said. "Just with a side of mild paranoia."

She made a face. "Remind me next year to go somewhere tropical."

"You'd last twelve hours without a working oven," I said.

"Rude," she said. "Accurate, but rude."

Back at the Morning Glory, the warmth hit us like a hug. The foyer smelled like pine and vanilla, and the tree in the parlor glowed in defiance of the missing star ten blocks away.

Sadie dropped the cinnamon votive at my feet like she'd solved the whole case. It rolled in a small circle and came to rest against my boot.

Barb leaned over her notebook, triumphant, as if the candle had just delivered a signed confession. "Day two," she announced. "Sabotage confirmed. Suspects: everyone."

Hannah groaned, unwinding her scarf. "It's going to be a long Christmas."

As I tucked the market gossip into my mental file labeled Noticing, I had to admit she was right. Christmas in

Marigold Lake had always been about lights and music and too many cookies.

This year, it was also going to be about shadows, missing stars, and a town full of people who suddenly weren't sure who they could trust.

And somewhere out there, I felt certain, someone was watching the whole thing unfold and enjoying every minute of it.

Chapter Three

The Morning Glory Merry Band

The Morning Glory was never quiet in December.

Between the guests, the decorations, and the constant hum of cookie sheets sliding in and out of the oven, the B&B felt like it had downed three candy canes and a gallon of cocoa. The walls practically vibrated with carols, conversation, and the occasional crash that meant Hannah had "adjusted" another baking experiment.

By mid-morning, she had commandeered the kitchen in a blizzard of flour and the kind of determination usually reserved for Olympic athletes and people trying to assemble furniture without instructions. The air smelled of cinnamon and cloves, punctuated by the occasional whiff of something slightly... overenthusiastic.

A tray of gingerbread men cooled on the counter, their heads lopsided, while another tray of snowmen looked like survivors of a volcanic eruption.

"Don't say it," Hannah warned, brandishing her spatula like a sword.

"I wasn't going to say anything."

"You were thinking it." She narrowed her eyes. "That they look like snowmen who just crawled out of Mount Vesuvius."

"Well..."

She smacked the counter with the spatula. Sadie barked once from her post by the pantry, as if to say, She's right, you know.

"Fine." Hannah sighed and reached for a piping bag. "I'll give them scarves. People forgive anything if you slap on accessories."

"Spoken like Barb," I said.

"Don't summon her," Hannah muttered.

Too late.

Barb swept in at that very moment, wrapped in a tartan scarf that could have doubled as a picnic blanket, cheeks pink from the cold, arms full of poinsettias. Glitter clung to her like she'd rolled through a craft aisle.

"Have you heard?" she demanded, dropping the plants onto the sideboard in a puff of red leaves. "The nativity scene is missing Baby Jesus!"

Hannah groaned. "You're kidding."

"Would I joke about divine kidnappings?" Barb pressed a hand to her chest. "First the star, now this. Next thing you know, the choir will be lip-syncing and Santa will be on strike."

"Maybe it was the wind," I offered, because denial is a valid coping mechanism.

"The wind doesn't waltz off with a plaster infant," Barb snapped. "Mark my words, Claire Fisher—this is sabotage. And I, for one, will not stand by while Maple Valley declares war on Christmas."

"Maybe check your sources before you declare war," I said.

"My source is Marjorie Spence, whose nephew dates the cousin of the man who drives the nativity truck. That's practically sworn testimony," Barb shot back.

Before I could argue with her version of the justice system, a clatter sounded from the hallway. Finn appeared ladder-first, muttering at a tangled strand of twinkle lights. His toolbox overflowed with wires, fuses, and three gadgets that looked like props from a sci-fi movie.

"Don't talk to me," he warned, eyes wild. "This strand is a traitor. Works in the kitchen, dies in the hallway, then flickers like a bad disco in the parlor. I'm five minutes from reprogramming it to spell SOS."

"Finn," I said carefully, "maybe take a break?"

"Breaks are for cowards." He jabbed the screwdriver at the lights. "If Maple Valley hacked our timers, I'll find them."

Barb gasped. "You think they could?"

"No," I said quickly. "Absolutely not."

Finn looked less certain. "Well... probably not. Unless they've got better Wi-Fi."

"Don't give Barb material," I whispered.

Too late again.

Barb straightened, eyes shining. "Cyber sabotage. I knew it. This is bigger than Baby Jesus. This is infrastructure."

"Please stop talking about Baby Jesus and infrastructure in the same sentence," Hannah begged.

Before anyone could escalate to a full Christmas conspiracy summit, the Millers—our retired road-tripping guests—bustled into the kitchen. Mrs. Miller carried her knitting bag like a weapon; Mr. Miller clutched his travel mug with the grim resignation of a man who had endured too many motel breakfasts.

"Terrible business about the nativity," Mrs. Miller said, settling into a chair like she'd just claimed it for Ohio. "Back home, someone once stole a wise man. But never Baby Jesus. That's new."

Her husband nodded gravely. "Maple Valley."

"See?" Barb crowed. "Even out-of-towners know."

"It could've been pranksters," I tried again.

"Pranksters don't haul off holy relics," Mr. Miller declared.

Sadie sneezed, which I chose to interpret as agreement with... whoever would end this conversation fastest.

The Petersons breezed in next, still in matching Christmas sweaters and still bickering like it was a competitive sport.

"Maple Valley's festival has more lights," Mrs. Peterson said, unloading a container of fudge onto the counter.

"More lights don't mean better," her husband retorted. "Ours has history."

"History doesn't make cocoa taste good."

"Neither does your attitude."

I rushed over with a plate of gingerbread men before they could divorce over dessert. "Here! Cookies fix everything."

They accepted the cookies, though their glares didn't soften much. Progress, not perfection.

From the doorway, a boy of about eight—another guest's grandson—announced proudly, "I think elves took Baby Jesus. To make him king of the North Pole!"

"That's... creative," I said.

Barb clapped. "See? Even the children sense a plot."

Sadie took this moment to jump up at the sideboard, knocking over one of Barb's poinsettias. Soil scattered across the rug like a crime scene.

"Sabotage!" Barb yelped. "They're targeting my plants now."

"Or maybe your plant was targeted by gravity," Hannah muttered, grabbing a broom.

The room dissolved into overlapping voices:

Mrs. Miller offering to knit a replacement Baby Jesus, complete with historically inaccurate scarf.

Mr. Miller demanding to know if Maple Valley even had poinsettias or if they just painted broccoli red.

The Petersons resuming their cocoa feud.

The eight-year-old loudly insisting elves had accomplices.

In the middle of it all, Finn yanked another cord from his toolbox and muttered, "If the lights so much as flicker, I'm wiring the whole block to a car battery."

"Please don't," I said. "I'm not sure 'Holiday B&B Electrocutes Town' is the press we're going for."

Hannah rolled her eyes so hard I thought they might stick. She yanked open the pantry, then froze.

The shelves where sacks of flour and cartons of butter should've been stacked were nearly bare. A half-bag of flour slumped in the corner beside three lonely sticks of butter. A single bag of sugar listed to the side like it had given up on life.

Her voice cracked. "Claire. My delivery never came."

The chatter around us blurred. I stepped to her side and peered into the pantry. Cold, practical panic nipped at my neck.

"Hannah, maybe they dropped it at the wrong door?" I said. "The inn across the street, or the coffee shop?"

She shook her head, curls bouncing. "I checked on my way in. Nobody's seen a delivery truck. I was supposed to get thirty pounds of flour, ten of sugar, twelve pounds of butter, and three cases of cream. Claire, I can't bake two hundred sugar cookies with this. This isn't rationing during wartime—it's Christmas."

Barb clutched her poinsettia like it was Exhibit A. "Sabotage on a dairy-and-grain level. This is war."

"Or a shipping error," I tried.

Hannah looked at me, and I saw beneath the flour and sarcasm—the tightness around her eyes, the way her shoulders had slowly hunched over the last week.

"Hey," I said softly. "We'll fix it. You're Hannah of the Twelve-Tray Cookie Miracle. You once catered a wedding with a mixer that only worked when someone kicked it every five minutes."

She huffed a laugh that sounded dangerously close to a sob. "That was you kicking it."

"We're a team," I said. "We'll be a team for this too."

Behind us, guests drifted closer, drawn by the change in Hannah's tone and the words "delivery never came" like sharks to emotional chum.

"I saw a truck idling near the square last night," one man offered. "About nine. Seemed odd."

"I heard jingling bells outside my window at midnight," a woman insisted.

"Elves," the eight-year-old chimed in again. "Definitely elves."

"Enough," Hannah said, scrubbing flour off her hands. "I need answers, not elf conspiracies."

Finn tapped his laptop like a detective presenting Exhibit A. "If I can get the delivery company's GPS logs, I might see where the truck stopped. Unless the saboteur hacked it."

Barb gasped. "They hacked Santa's supply chain!"

"No one hacked Santa," I said firmly. "Santa is unhackable."

"Speak for yourself," Finn muttered, already typing.

The kitchen fell into a tense hush as we gathered around Finn like he was about to reveal the winning lottery numbers. He chewed his lip, fingers flying over the keys, the glow from the screen painting his face an anxious blue.

"How do you even have access to their GPS?" I whispered.

He shrugged one shoulder. "They have a customer portal. And a security hole you could drive a reindeer team through. I'm doing them a favor."

"That's... not how favors work," I said.

Barb leaned so far over his shoulder her scarf nearly smothered Sadie. "Enhance," she whispered dramatically.

"That's not a real thing," Finn said through his teeth. "This isn't CSI: Marigold."

Another minute ticked by. The oven timer beeped. Hannah ignored it. Somewhere in the house a guest laughed at something on TV like we weren't standing in the kitchen watching Christmas crumble.

"Got it," Finn said finally. "Okay. The truck left Cedar Falls at six p.m., moved normally, hit the interstate, turned off at Marigold Lake... and—" His grin faded. "It stopped. For twenty-seven minutes. Not at the B&B, not at the market. At the edge of town. Near the old skating pond."

The room went still. Even Barb stopped scribbling.

"Why there?" Hannah whispered.

Finn turned the laptop so we could see a little map of town, studded with labeled points he'd added himself: Morning Glory, Square, Maple Valley Turnoff. A blinking red dot sat just beyond the last houses, near a patch of white that represented the pond and surrounding woods.

"Could be they pulled off to rest," I said, though my voice lacked conviction. "Or got stuck."

"If they got stuck, they'd call," Hannah said. "And they wouldn't be 'stuck' for twenty-seven minutes and then vanish off the route."

"Maybe they unloaded something," Barb said, eyes alight. "At a secret rendezvous point."

"Could be a mechanical problem," Mr. Miller suggested. "I used to drive a truck. Sometimes you pull over, kick a tire, say bad words, then keep going."

"But they never kept going," Hannah said. "That's the problem. The status on my order is 'delivered.'"

The knot in my stomach tightened. "Delivered where?" I asked Finn.

He clicked. "It just says: Marigold Lake, IA. Signed by: M. Garland."

"Garland?" I repeated. "We don't have a Garland on staff. Or a Garland at the B&B. Unless the wreaths have started signing for packages."

Hannah looked stricken. "Claire, that's the flour, sugar, butter, cream... my entire holiday baking arsenal."

43

Hannah didn't talk about it often, but I knew more than she thought I did. About how, after her divorce, she'd moved back to Marigold Lake with nothing but a car full of cookbooks and a half-broken mixer. How the first Christmas she'd baked for the Morning Glory, she'd cried behind the pantry door because a guest's offhand "just like store-bought" had cut deeper than it should.

Now she poured everything into these desserts. Every cookie was another little declaration: I stayed. I rebuilt. I can do this.

And now someone had taken her supplies like they were just... things.

Sadie gave a sharp bark and bounded toward the back door like she was ready to drag us to the pond herself.

"Woof," said the eight-year-old gravely. "She says we should investigate."

"Of course she does," Barb said. "She's a sleuth. It's in her blood. Probably."

I forced my brain to push past the emotional part. "Okay. We're not marching to the pond right this minute. We'll give this to Matt. He can call the company, check the driver, figure out if this Garland person is real or a very seasonal alias."

Barb's eyes sparkled. "Oho. A Christmas-themed criminal. Diabolical."

"Sounds like your dream date," Hannah muttered.

Laughter flickered, weak but present. The kitchen relaxed by half a notch.

"All right," I said, falling into host mode because that was something I could still control. "Game plan. Finn, send that GPS log to Matt. Hannah, can you triage what you can still make with what we've got? I'll call around and see who has surplus flour and butter. Maybe the diner or the church kitchen can loan us some."

"I'll ask Mrs. Palmer," Mrs. Miller offered. "She travels with emergency baking supplies. Says you never know when a pie will call to you."

"See?" Barb said, triumphant. "The merry band assembles."

"The what?" I asked.

She flourished her pen. "The Morning Glory Merry Band. That's what I'm calling us in my notes. Every investigation needs a colorful supporting cast."

"Fantastic," I said. "Do we get matching capes?"

Hannah snorted. "If there are capes, I want mine flour-resistant."

Finn was already typing again. "I can set up a shared drive," he said. "Pictures, notes, logs, anything suspicious. Think of it as a digital corkboard of chaos."

"Finn," I said, "please don't say 'shared drive' to Barb. She'll try to print it."

"I heard that," Barb huffed. "And I absolutely will. Evidence belongs on paper. Paper has gravitas."

The kitchen began to hum again—still tense, but moving. Mugs clinked. The oven timer pinged. Hannah grabbed a notepad and started scribbling backup recipes that used less butter. It was like watching a general reorganize troops after a surprise attack.

"Claire?" Mrs. Miller said gently, catching my sleeve as the others drifted back to their tasks. "Is this... normal? For your Christmases here?"

"Normal?" I repeated. "No. Typical? Maybe."

She smiled kindly. "You're handling it well."

What I wanted to say was: I am hanging on by a tinsel thread. What I said was, "We've had... practice."

She nodded knowingly. "Town like this? Folks have long memories and short fuses. But they also have big hearts." She patted my hand. "Don't let them forget that part."

I watched her rejoin her husband, who was now giving the eight-year-old an earnest lecture on the theological implications of elf-based kidnappings, and something eased in my chest.

"Claire." Hannah's voice tugged me back. "I'm going to improvise. Lemon bars instead of sugar cookies. I've got enough eggs and sugar for a few batches."

"Those are a hit," I said. "Remember last year when the mayor ate five and then tried to declare a town holiday called Citrus Appreciation Day?"

She managed a smile. "I'll make extra. Stress baking helps."

"Good," I said. "Bake us through the apocalypse."

Finn slid past with his ladder, almost decapitating a snow-man cookie. "Reminder: if the lights flicker, it's probably me, not the saboteur."

"Comforting," I said.

As the crowd thinned, I slipped into the hallway with Finn's laptop under my arm and the GPS image still burned into my mind. Old Skating Pond. Twenty-seven minutes. Garland.

I paused by the front window. Outside, snow drifted down in slow, soft curtains. Across the street, the square looked deceptively peaceful. Tree bare at the top, nativity missing a baby, but volunteers still moving through the scene, sweeping, rehanging, trying.

Trying mattered.

Behind me, Sadie trotted up and pressed her head against my calf. I scratched behind her ears. "What do you think, girl? Maple Valley? Bored teenagers? Rogue elves?"

She gave me a look that said, Don't be ridiculous, and flicked her gaze toward the porch like she expected someone to be standing there.

"Okay," I said quietly. "We'll keep our eyes open. We'll help where we can. And we'll tell Matt everything—before Barb decides to launch Operation Baby Jesus."

From the kitchen came the sound of Hannah's mixer starting up again, louder and steadier this time. Barb's voice floated through the doorway: "Chapter Three: The Merry Band Mobilizes."

I shook my head, but I couldn't help smiling.

For all the chaos—missing stars, vanished deliveries, plaster babies on the lam—one thing was true: I wasn't facing it alone. I had a band, whether I'd signed up for one or not.

"Come on, Sadie," I said, turning back toward the noise and the warmth and the flour-stormed battlefield. "If someone's waging war on Christmas, they picked the wrong town."

Chapter Four

Pancakes, Panic and Prying Questions

Breakfast at the Morning Glory was never a calm affair, but this morning it felt like someone had swapped the maple syrup for jet fuel.

The dining room buzzed with overlapping conversations, the clatter of cutlery, and the faint hiss of bacon from the kitchen. The air smelled of cinnamon pancakes and strong coffee—normally enough to calm a crowd. Not today. Today, every whisper sounded like a theory and every dropped fork like the start of a riot.

Snow feathered against the front windows, blurring Main Street into soft white. Inside, the Morning Glory pulsed with color: red napkins, green runner on the buffet, silver coffee urns, and a Christmas tree in the corner dripping with ornaments that Barb had declared "tastefully excessive."

At table one, the Petersons were locked in their usual duel.

"Your pancake is too doughy," Mrs. Peterson sniffed, poking at it like it had offended her ancestors.

"Your attitude is too sour," Mr. Peterson snapped back. "Maybe you're confusing the two."

They'd been married thirty years, from what they'd told me. Apparently, twenty-nine of those had been fueled entirely by passive-aggressive breakfast commentary.

At table two, the Millers leaned in like spies in witness protection. Mrs. Miller's knitting needles clacked under the table, her eyes sparkling with scandal.

"We heard the star wasn't stolen by Maple Valley at all," she whispered. "Word is, a local did it."

"Locals always do it," Mr. Miller muttered into his coffee, as if this were a proven law of physics. "Nobody travels across state lines to ruin a perfectly good nativity."

At table three, Doris Temple held court, glaring at the ceiling like she expected aliens to cut through the plaster at any moment.

"I'm telling you," she said, leaning forward. "They start with small symbolic objects. First the star, then the baby, next it'll be the Wise Men. It's always the scouts first."

"The scouts?" her neighbor repeated weakly.

"The aliens send advance scouts," Doris said. "It's in the documentaries. You just have to know where to stream them."

I wove between tables with a coffee pot in one hand and a basket of mini muffins in the other, refilling mugs and attempting my best impression of Switzerland—neutral, smiling, and hoping nobody threw syrup.

Sadie trotted close at my heels, wearing her red scarf like a badge of office. She paused dramatically by the buffet, stretched up on her hind legs, and tried to swipe a pancake. I caught her mid-snatch, lifting the plate out of reach.

"Not for you," I scolded. "You're on the clock."

She responded with an indignant sneeze that sprayed half the room.

"See?" Doris declared, dabbing at her glasses. "The dog knows! She's warning us about alien interference."

Sadie gave her a look that could only be translated as *ma'am, I just wanted carbs*.

From the kitchen, Hannah's voice floated out, riding a wave of sizzling bacon. "Claire! Do we have more butter? Guests are panicking in here!"

"Guests are panicking out here too," I muttered, topping off Mr. Miller's mug before it could become a weapon.

"Bless you," Mrs. Miller said, as if coffee refills could absolve me of whatever Marigold Lake thought I'd done to Christmas.

Barb barreled in then, her tartan scarf trailing like a battle flag and her notebook already open. Her lipstick was fresh, her cheeks were pink, and her energy level was somewhere between "election rally" and "game show host on finals week."

"Attention, citizens of Marigold Lake!" she announced, stepping in front of the pancake buffet like it was a podium. "The saboteur has escalated. We're not talking minor mischief anymore—we're talking targeted attacks on holiday morale."

The room quieted just enough for forks to hover mid-air. Even the Petersons paused mid-argument, which ranked somewhere near "rare astronomical event" on the local scale.

"Last night," Barb continued dramatically, "a reliable source informed me that a suspicious flour truck was seen circling the square. And this morning? Baby Jesus vanished from the nativity."

Gasps rippled. One guest actually clutched their pearls. Another dropped his fork with a clatter.

"Oh, for the love of..." I began.

"Coincidence?" Barb demanded. "I think not. This is organized sabotage, people, and I intend to get answers."

"Oh no," I whispered, too late.

Barb turned toward the nearest guest—a sweet college kid traveling with his grandmother—and stabbed her pencil in his direction like an accusatory wand.

"You," she said. "Where were you last night between ten and midnight?"

The poor kid nearly choked on his pancake. "Um... in bed?"

His grandmother swatted Barb with her napkin. "Don't interrogate my grandson before he finishes his breakfast. That's a crime."

Unfazed, Barb whirled toward the Millers. The tartan scarf swung dramatically, narrowly missing the syrup pitcher.

"And you! Ohio," she said, pointing at Mr. Miller as if the entire state were suspicious. "You drove in from out of town. Plenty of trunk space for a missing plaster infant."

"Lady," Mr. Miller said dryly, "I barely had room for my socks."

Mrs. Miller nodded. "He had to choose between his bowling shoes and his winter coat. The coat almost lost."

"Compromised luggage, suspicious priorities," Barb muttered, scribbling in her notebook. "Noted."

At the buffet, the Petersons joined in.

"Maple Valley," Mrs. Peterson announced, pointing her fork like a compass. "You mark my words. They're behind all of this."

"Maple Valley can't even salt their sidewalks properly," her husband replied. "You think they could pull off a heist? This has *homegrown* written all over it."

"Are you saying our own neighbors would steal Baby Jesus?"

"I'm saying our neighbors once stole my snowblower, so yes."

I pressed a hand to my forehead. Hannah emerged from the kitchen, flour streaked across her cheek, holding a tray of pancakes like a peace offering. Her ponytail had come half loose, and there was a dusting of powdered sugar in her hair that made her look like a stressed-out Christmas angel.

"Breakfast diplomacy," she muttered, sliding the tray onto the buffet. "May it calm the masses."

It didn't.

At the far table, the eight-year-old boy who'd been theorizing about elves leaned back in his chair and announced, "I think the elves took Baby Jesus. To make him king of the North Pole. It's how promotions work."

Doris gasped. "You see? Even the children *sense* a plot."

Sadie chose this moment to hop up against the sideboard, her front paws hitting the table just hard enough to knock over the sugar shaker. It rolled, tipped, and spilled a small mountain of sugar across the tablecloth.

"Sabotage!" Barb cried. "They're targeting condiments now!"

"Or maybe your plant was targeted by gravity yesterday and the sugar by canine ambition today," Hannah said, wiping sugar with a rag.

The room erupted again—voices layering over one another like badly mixed carols.

"I saw a truck idling by the church last night," someone said.

"I heard jingling outside my window," another insisted.

"That was the neighbor's wind chimes," her husband replied.

"Could've been part of the cover," she shot back.

"It's all connected," Doris declared. "First the star, then Baby Jesus, next..." She shuddered. "They'll take the reindeer from the hardware store roof. Then where will we be?"

"In a town with one less inflatable Rudolph," I said under my breath.

Finn wandered in then, carrying his laptop under one arm and a string of still-blinking lights under the other. His hair stood up like he'd lost a fight with static electricity. His toolbox clanked at his hip.

"Everyone relax," he announced, though his eye twitching suggested he was not, in fact, relaxed. "I pulled the porch cam footage."

Barb nearly dropped her notebook. "You have *footage*?"

Finn nodded, relishing his moment. He set the laptop on the sideboard and opened it like it was the Ark of the Covenant. "Guess what? At exactly 12:23 a.m., someone tall and hooded stood at the edge of the walk. They didn't come inside, but they lingered. Suspicious, right?"

The nearest guests crowded closer, craning to see a grainy, snow-flecked view of our front walk. A tall shape hovered at the edge of the camera's frame, just beyond the glow of the porch light.

A little shiver skated across my arms.

"How long did they stay?" I asked.

"Forty-three seconds," Finn said. "Long enough to stare at the wreath like it owed them money."

Barb made a strangled sound of triumph. "A suspect! This is our break!"

I squinted at the screen. The figure shifted, the hood turning, like whoever it was had glanced toward the square before walking away. It might've been nothing. It might've been everything.

"Could be a neighbor," I said. "Or someone checking the address."

"Or someone casing the place," Finn countered. "Or checking to see if the star's next."

The room erupted into speculation again. Doris Temple swore it was aliens in disguise "using a human host." The Petersons accused Maple Valley by committee. The Millers muttered about "locals, always locals." The eight-year-old shouted, "Elves!" and mimed tiny feet sneaking across the snow.

Sadie barked once, sharp and decisive, like she was voting too.

And there I was, standing in the middle of it all—coffee pot in one hand, pancake thief disguised as a Boston Terrier at my feet, and my B&B transformed into a courtroom without a judge.

"Okay!" I called, trying to sound like a woman completely in charge of her life and not like someone whose internal Christmas spirit was chewing its nails. "Refills anyone?"

Half the room thrust their mugs at me. The other half kept arguing. This was fine. This was normal.

The front door opened then, letting in a swirl of cold air and a few flakes of snow that swirled across the entryway rug. Matt stepped in, brushing snow from his coat, his gaze automatically sweeping the scene: guests arguing, Barb grandstanding, Finn mid-lecture, Hannah brandishing a spatula like a weapon. His eyes landed on me, and for a heartbeat I thought he might turn around and walk back out.

Instead, he sighed, the kind of sigh that could power a snowplow, and shut the door behind him.

"Claire," he said slowly, taking in the chaos. "Please tell me this is just breakfast."

"Breakfast," I said brightly, handing him a pancake from the tray Hannah shoved into my hands. "With a side of sabotage."

He arched a brow. "Of course."

I passed him a steaming mug of coffee. The corner of his mouth softened as he wrapped his hands around it. He looked tired—dark circles under his eyes, jaw tight—but when he looked at me, some of that tension eased.

"What's the damage?" he asked quietly, leaning closer so his voice wouldn't carry.

"Verbal accusations, minor sugar spill, no physical injuries," I said. "Unless you count Hannah's blood pressure."

"Hey!" Hannah called from the kitchen. "My blood pressure is perfectly respectable."

"She's lying," I murmured.

He huffed out a laugh, then brushed a smudge of flour from my cheek with his thumb. The touch was quick, casual, but it sent a warm spark through my chest that had nothing to do with the coffee.

"You always get caught in the middle, don't you?" he said.

"Occupational hazard," I replied. "B&B owner, unofficial town therapist, part-time saboteur wrangler."

He took a slow sip of coffee, studying the room. "I talked to the pastor on my way over. Baby Jesus wasn't just missing this morning. He was gone sometime between ten last night and six this morning. No footprints they can distinguish from the rest. Just... gone."

"So whoever took the star might be the same person?" I asked.

"Maybe." His gaze drifted toward the tree in the corner of the dining room, where a handmade star from one of Barb's Bunco nights perched at the top, a placeholder until the town found the real one—or bought a new one and pretended they didn't care. "Or maybe we've got more than one prankster who doesn't know when to quit."

Barb swooped in, unable to handle being left out of a conversation for more than three seconds. "Detective Hale, I have identified at least three suspects since eight-thirty."

"Of course you have," Matt said.

"One," she said, ticking off fingers, "the Millers. Drifters from Ohio with ambiguous sock storage. Two, the Petersons. They spend an alarming amount of time arguing about Maple Valley. Guilty conscience? And three—" she lowered her voice, "—I heard from Marjorie Spence that someone anonymous donated a large sum to Maple Valley's decorating fund last week. Anonymous donations always mean guilt."

"Or generosity," I said.

"Or laundering, but that's for the movies," Barb replied. "Anyway, I'm working on a suspect board."

Matt pinched the bridge of his nose. "Please don't put a suspect board in the parlor again."

"That was one time," Barb scoffed. "And it was tasteful."

"You used glitter glue to write 'WHO DONE IT,'" he said.

"That's branding."

Behind us, Sadie hopped onto an empty chair and fixed Matt with a hard stare until he broke off a corner of pancake and handed it down.

"Accomplice," he muttered.

She chewed loudly, unbothered.

Hannah slipped out of the kitchen, wiping her hands on her apron. Her forehead pinched as she caught my eye. "Any updates on my missing delivery?" she asked Matt.

"We tracked the truck on GPS," Matt said. "The driver claims he dropped everything at the service entrance."

Hannah's eyes widened. "The service entrance that leads to... nowhere?"

"Exactly," I said. "We don't *have* a service entrance. We have a back door and a cranky raccoon who occasionally files noise complaints."

Matt nodded. "We're working on it. The company's sending over their internal logs. It could be a clerical error, but..." His eyes met mine. "After the star and the nativity, I'm not in the mood to give anyone the benefit of the doubt."

"Welcome to Barb's world," Barb said. "We've been out of benefits for years."

"Barb," I said gently, "maybe let Matt handle the official investigation."

"Of course," she said loftily. "I'm just running the unofficial one. That's where the *real* breakthroughs happen."

Matt muttered something under his breath about moving to Florida.

I touched his arm. "We'll send you the porch cam footage," I said. "And Finn's GPS screenshot from the flour truck."

Finn perked up. "Already in your inbox, Detective. With annotations. And emojis so you know which parts are alarming."

Matt closed his eyes for a second, like he was silently asking the universe for strength. "Thanks, Finn."

"Anytime," Finn said proudly. "This is like Christmas meets cybercrime. It's my time to shine."

"Please don't actually shine anything," Hannah called. "No more sparks out of outlets, I mean it."

Matt squeezed my shoulder lightly. "I'll update you when I know more. In the meantime..." His gaze swept the room again, catching on Doris, the Petersons, the eight-year-old now stacking syrup packets into a fort. "Try to keep the panic down?"

"I make no promises," I said. "But I'll keep the pancakes coming."

He hesitated, then leaned in just enough that his breath warmed my ear. "And Claire?"

"Yeah?"

"If you hear anything—see anything—call me before Barb deputizes half the town."

"Too late," Barb sang from across the room. "The Bunco brigade is already on high alert."

Matt looked at me. I looked at him. We both sighed.

He took his coffee to a corner table, pulling out his small notebook as he started writing. Even off-duty, he couldn't help it. Detective Hale didn't stop being Detective Hale just because his pancakes came with powdered sugar.

Breakfast at the Morning Glory wasn't just pancakes anymore. It was chaos, clues, suspects, and the dawning realization that whoever was messing with our town knew exactly where to hit us: our traditions, our symbols, and now our sense of safety.

I refilled another mug, nudged Sadie away from a plate she'd decided to "guard," and caught my reflection in the dining room window—hair slightly frizzed, flour on my sleeve, worry in my eyes.

"Okay," I murmured to myself. "Breakfast first. Then sleuthing."

Sadie nudged my ankle like she agreed.

Matt looked up from his notes and met my gaze across the room. Something steady passed between us—part exasperation, part determination, part *here we go again*.

And as snow swirled outside and the Morning Glory buzzed with speculation, I knew one thing for sure: this wasn't just breakfast.

This was the beginning of our case.

Chapter Five

Guest Spotlight at the Morning Glory

If the Morning Glory had a personality, it was a magpie—always collecting stories, gossip, and the occasional shiny object left behind in a dresser drawer. And this morning, the parlor was practically cackling with secrets.

Our guests were supposed to be enjoying a calm holiday getaway. Instead, they were treating my B&B like the set of a reality show called *Suspicion in Snow Boots.*

The Petersons had commandeered the wingback chairs near the fireplace, arguing over whose cocoa had the better marshmallow-to-liquid ratio.

"**It's watery**," Mrs. Peterson complained, flicking a marshmallow with the tip of her spoon.

"**It's festive**," her husband countered. "You can't measure joy in ounces. You have to feel it."

Across the room, the Millers sat shoulder-to-shoulder with a crossword book between them, loudly debating whether **"yule log"** could possibly count as a six-letter clue for *holiday dessert.*

"It's two words," Mrs. Miller insisted.

"Crosswords don't care about rules," her husband said. "They just want your soul."

At the game table, Doris Temple rummaged through her binoculars and highlighters. "I saw *hooded figures* at the lamppost at three a.m.," she announced.

"Doris," her neighbor Marjorie Spence sighed, "that was the paperboy. Again."

"Paperboys don't lurk," Doris insisted. "They skulk. Very different energy."

I set a plate of scones on the coffee table and tried to summon calm through carbohydrates. "Let's remember we're here to relax," I said, with a smile that felt like it was held together with masking tape.

"Relax?" Barb repeated, sweeping into the room like someone had fired her out of a tinsel cannon. "Relax while saboteurs roam free?"

She snapped open her notebook with the gravity of an FBI agent.

"No, Claire," she continued. "We must observe. We must interrogate. We must—"

"Eat a scone," I said, shoving one into her hand before she could start assigning code names.

Barb bit into it like it was evidence. "Fine. But chewing improves focus."

Sadie made rounds between chairs, her red scarf bobbing like a tiny marching banner. When Mrs. Peterson dropped a marshmallow, Sadie inhaled it whole and strutted like she'd earned a medal of valor.

Then the doorbell chimed.

Hannah appeared, cheeks flushed and a dusting of flour on one eyebrow. "Claire, more guests!"

In swept a woman in a green velvet coat and heels that had definitely never encountered Iowa slush. She gazed around the parlor like it was an audition space.

"**Leona Brandt**," she declared. "Writer. Lifestyle essays, mostly. I require quiet for inspiration and three cups of tea daily, with lemon. *Fresh* lemon."

Barb gasped. "A writer! Perfect. She can chronicle Maple Valley's sabotage plot for posterity."

Leona blinked. "Excuse me?"

"Don't mind her," I said quickly. "Welcome to the Morning Glory."

Behind Leona came a middle-aged man with a camera and the expression of someone who found joy in dusty archives.

"Tourist?" I asked hopefully.

"**Historian**," he corrected. "Frank Danner. I collect small-town holiday lore. The real stuff—rituals, lost traditions, regional quirks. May I photograph that garland? It has period accuracy."

He pointed his lens toward Sadie. "And the dog. She seems iconic."

Sadie straightened like she'd spent years preparing for this exact moment.

While I checked them in, the parlor noise swelled like a storm cloud gathering drama.

Within minutes:

Leona was explaining the emotional significance of tea temperature

Frank was interviewing Barb about "historic patterns of festive sabotage"

Doris was loudly insisting aliens probably had a taste for plaster

Marjorie was threatening to confiscate Doris's binoculars

The Millers were still arguing about crossword validity

The Petersons were now auditing *each other's* cocoa ratios by teaspoon

It was less like running a B&B and more like babysitting a troop of caffeinated reindeer.

Hannah returned with a tray of miniature muffins. "Your guests are… lively," she whispered.

"Lively is good," I said weakly. "As long as they don't riot before checkout."

But the truth hit me all at once:
This wasn't background noise anymore.

The guests were becoming **part of the mystery.**
Witnesses. Suspects. Distractions. Story fuel.
A whole cast of characters dropped into my lap like the

universe had decided to stage a Christmas play in my living room.

"Claire," Leona called from across the parlor, "does your cocoa always have a... poetic thinness?"

"It's not thin," Hannah snapped. "It's airy."

Frank scribbled in his notebook. "Airy cocoa... intriguing."

"Oh no," I whispered. "We're becoming folklore."

The doorbell chimed again.

A tall man stepped inside—lean, bundled, with a stern expression that suggested he hadn't smiled in five years.

"Name?" I asked kindly.

"**Colton Parrish**," he said, brushing snow from his coat. "I'm here visiting a—" He paused. "Friend."

Something in his tone made my radar ping.
Hannah noticed too; she cast me a sideways glance.

"Will you be staying long?" I asked.

"Not if I can help it."
His eyes darted toward the parlor guests, lingering a beat too long on Frank's camera.

Sadie padded over and sniffed Colton's boots, then backed up slowly—her version of a raised eyebrow.

"We have rooms available," I said.

He hesitated. "Fine."

As I checked him in, Barb strutted over, notebook poised. "Any chance you know anything about missing stars, nativity pieces, or flour shipments?"

Colton didn't even blink. "No."

Barb narrowed her eyes. "Suspicious."

"Don't mind her," I said again—my new catchphrase. "Breakfast is at eight."

"Breakfast," he repeated, like the word was foreign.

When he turned away, Hannah leaned in. "Claire... that guy has the energy of someone who bought coal on purpose."

"He's probably tired," I said.

"He looks like a man who broods recreationally."

She wasn't wrong.

But before I could say more, chaos erupted again.

Doris shrieked, "THE WISE MEN ARE NEXT!"

The Petersons began arguing about cocoa density.

Frank took a photo of the poinsettia like it held answers.

Leona complained the muffled chatter "interfered with her creative chakra."

And Barb declared, "Saboteur count now includes EIGHT potential suspects!"

Sadie jumped into my lap, breath warm against my hand.

"Well, girl," I murmured, looking out over the chaotic parlor, "looks like we've got our full cast."

Sadie thumped her nub tail once—firm, decisive.

As if to say:

And I'm the star.

Chapter Six

Supplies and Suspicions

The Morning Glory was buzzing with more tension than cheer. Hannah paced in front of the pantry like a general surveying a battlefield. Her flour-dusted sneakers squeaked against the tile, a sound that somehow made everything feel more dire.

"This is a disaster," she muttered, slapping her baking notebook onto the counter. "My marathon baking day is ruined before it's even begun. No flour, no butter—how am I supposed to pull off pecan tassies, shortbread, and cinnamon stars with this? The only thing I'll be serving is a platter of panic."

Barb's eyes gleamed like she'd been waiting for such an announcement since July. She slapped her notebook onto the counter so its pages splayed dramatically. "Not ruined—sabotaged. First the star, then Baby Jesus, and now your pantry. This isn't an accident, Claire. We've moved into dairy warfare. This is holiday war."

"Barb," I said, rubbing my temple, "not every problem comes with a Maple Valley return address."

"Tell that to their mayor," Barb sniffed. "Shifty eyes, that one. And their choir wears matching capes like they're auditioning for *Dracula on Ice*."

Hannah threw her hands up. "Please! While you two debate vampires, I have two hundred cookies to make. If I don't get flour and butter now, I'll have to pipe frosting onto my tears and call it dessert."

Sadie barked once, then padded toward the mudroom and pawed at the door like she knew exactly what needed to be done. Her nub tail flicked with purpose.

"She's right," I sighed. "Emergency store run. Coats on, everyone. Let's move."

Getting my merry band out the door was like organizing a circus parade. Barb insisted on swapping her tartan scarf for a red plaid one because "interrogations require the proper armor." Hannah clutched her baking notebook like it was a survival manual. Finn strapped on his flashlight and a multi-tool "just in case the store's electrical system is compromised."

By the time we piled into my SUV, Sadie had claimed the passenger seat, planted square and proud, as if she'd been named official navigator. Her breath puffed tiny clouds onto the window.

"You realize," Barb announced as we pulled out of the drive, "this is Maple Valley's fault."

"Barb," I warned.

"They've bribed delivery drivers before, I can feel it. It's common knowledge rival towns hoard butter during holiday seasons."

"That is not common knowledge," Hannah said sharply.

"Look it up," Barb muttered.

Finn leaned over from the back seat. "Please don't. That's how conspiracy blogs are born."

Sadie sneezed like she agreed with him.

The grocery store parking lot was a blur of slush, holiday traffic, and bundled-up shoppers marching with the grim determination of soldiers on the front line of seasonal chaos. My windshield wipers groaned against the snow like they were questioning my life choices.

Inside, the store smelled like cinnamon brooms and wet wool, and the aisles throbbed with carts colliding, Christmas music on loop, and children begging for candy canes with the tenacity of professional negotiators.

Hannah made a beeline for the baking aisle. "Please, please, please," she chanted under her breath. A moment later she let out a cry of relief and hoisted a sack of flour like a trophy. "We're saved!"

"Temporarily," Finn muttered, hauling it into the cart. "You'll need at least four more."

Hannah grabbed them all, tossing bags like a woman arming for war. A nearby shopper sidestepped as if dodging artillery.

Barb, meanwhile, had cornered the teenage cashier restocking candy canes.

"Tell me everything you know about the missing deliveries. Who delayed them? Who benefits from butter shortages? Don't hold back."

The boy blinked at her, slack-jawed. "Uh... ma'am, I just put candy on shelves."

"Exactly!" Barb hissed, scribbling in her notebook. "The perfect cover."

Over by the butter case, Hannah's voice rose again. "Claire! Do you see these prices? Outrageous. They're practically charging in bullion." She stuffed cartons into the cart anyway. "Don't judge me. Desperate bakers can't be choosers."

Finn wandered toward self-checkout and started poking at the screen. "Their system's outdated. I could reprogram it to play carols."

"Don't," I said firmly, steering him back toward the group.

Sadie, trotting happily on her leash, stopped dead at a towering snowman display. She planted her paws, hackles half-raised, and issued a growl so dramatic it echoed down the aisle. Then she launched into full bark mode.

The inflatable snowman wobbled dangerously into a stack of peppermint bark tins.

I lunged and steadied it, narrowly avoiding an avalanche of chocolate and broken pride.

"See?" Barb said, pointing dramatically. "Even the dog knows villainy when she sees it!"

The store manager—a round man with a pencil mustache—hurried over, puffing. "Everything all right?"

"We're fine," I said quickly, righting the display.

"Not fine," Hannah corrected, waving her butter like Exhibit A. "Our delivery never came. Flour, sugar, butter—gone."

The man groaned. "You and everyone else. We've had half-empty trucks for a week now. No word from the depot, no explanation. It's the strangest thing."

Barb gasped. "Proof of sabotage!"

"Or," the man said, "the supply chain's a mess."

"Same thing," Barb muttered darkly.

As we turned toward the checkout, an older woman bumped into our cart, apologized, then lowered her voice conspiratorially.

"Be careful," she whispered. "My cousin in Pine Ridge says their entire bakery shipment vanished last night. No tracks. No explanation."

Barb slapped her notebook open so fast it startled the woman. "Name? Time? Weather conditions? Were capes involved?"

I gently steered her away.

By the time we checked out, our cart looked like we were provisioning for a blizzard—or an apocalypse. Flour towered over the edge. Butter bricks jostled dangerously. Hannah hovered like a hawk, muttering about ratios and schedules.

Back at the B&B, we unloaded the haul into the kitchen. Hannah immediately launched into prep mode, measuring flour with military precision as classical Christmas music drifted from the radio. Her shoulders loosened with every scoop.

Finn disappeared to wrestle with the hall lights again, muttering about "suspicious surges."

Barb parked herself at the counter, notebook open, writing a suspect list titled *The Butter Bandits*. She included everyone from Maple Valley's mayor to the produce clerk at the market.

For a moment, the parlor glowed like nothing was wrong: twinkle lights, cocoa mugs, guests laughing in overstuffed chairs. It almost felt like Christmas again.

Then Sadie froze, planted her paws at the window, and let out that same sharp growl.

My heart stumbled.

I joined her and peered out into the snowy evening. A dark SUV idled at the corner, headlights dimmed, exhaust curling white into the night. The figure inside sat still—too still—like they were watching rather than waiting.

"Whose car is that?" I murmured.

Finn came down the stairs, wiping his hands on a rag. He squinted through the glass. "Plates look like Maple Valley."

The SUV lingered just long enough to prickle the hairs on my neck, then rolled away into the snow-dimmed dusk.

"Caught in the act!" Barb cried.

"In the act of driving?" I asked.

"Driving suspiciously!"

The unease clung even after the door shut against the cold. A knock rattled the wood a moment later.

Barb gasped, clutching her scarf. "They've come for us!"

Finn opened the door before she could spiral further.

Matt stepped inside, stamping snow from his boots, his dark peacoat dusted with fresh flakes. His expression was calm, but edged with weariness—the look of someone who'd fielded too many panicked calls and not enough coffee.

"Evening," he said, his voice deep enough to settle the room. "I'm guessing you all saw the SUV."

"Maple Valley plates!" Barb declared. "Claire nearly fainted!"

"I did not," I muttered, though my pulse was still thudding.

Matt arched a brow but let it pass. "We've had three calls tonight about strange vehicles and missing decorations. The star and Baby Jesus are officially on my desk now." He sighed, running a hand through his hair. "I don't love it, but it's my job to keep this from turning into a full-on holiday riot."

"Maple Valley is guilty," Barb said firmly.

"Maybe," Matt said evenly. "Or maybe someone here enjoys stirring the pot. Either way, I'll handle it." His gaze softened when it landed on me. "And you'll let me, right?"

I smiled thinly. "We'll... notice. Carefully."

He gave the slow blink of a man who knew exactly what that meant. Then, leaning closer so only I could hear, he murmured, "Not everything broken can be fixed with gingerbread."

His glance dropped to the flour dusting my sleeve, softening just a little more. "Even you can't bake this one back together."

Sadie pawed at his boot like she agreed.

I wanted to promise I'd stay out of it—that I'd let him handle the case while I stuck to cocoa and check-ins. But as I looked around—the flour-streaked Hannah, the sparking Finn, Barb scribbling her manifesto—I knew I couldn't.

"I'll try," I said.

Matt exhaled like he'd expected nothing less. Then he bent to scratch Sadie's ears. "That's what I was afraid of."

And somewhere outside, beneath the snowy hush, I swear I felt the saboteur winding up their next move.

Chapter Seven

Bunco and Bad Tidings

Barb's house looked like Santa's workshop had been swallowed whole by a glitter bomb.

Garland wrapped the stair rail, poinsettias crowded every flat surface, and her dining table gleamed beneath a sequined runner that could've doubled as a landing strip for reindeer. The whole house smelled like nutmeg, tinsel, and the faint metallic tang of someone who owned far too much glitter glue.

"This night will be historic," Barb whispered as she fussed with a stack of score sheets. Her eyes glittered with the zeal of a woman already drafting tomorrow's headline: **Local Heroine Solves Christmas Sabotage Between Dice Rolls.**

"I thought we were just playing Bunco," I said, balancing a tray of Hannah's cookies.

Barb patted my arm like I was a child who didn't yet understand the world's complexities. "Claire, Bunco is always cover for intelligence gathering. Ask anyone."

"I'm not sure 'anyone' agrees with you."

"Anyone *wise*," Barb corrected.

Her living room was crammed with folding card tables, crockpots bubbling on the sideboard, and two dozen women in sweaters that ranged from modest snowflakes to full-on battery-powered Santas. The air buzzed with chatter, cinnamon cider, canned laughter from the holiday movie playing softly in the background, and the faint whiff of crockpot meatballs threatening to burn.

Sadie trotted under the tables like a four-legged referee, ready to enforce snack distribution. She wore her red scarf proudly, as if Barb had formally deputized her.

Finn crouched in the corner with a portable speaker, muttering at it like it had personally wronged him. "Play carols. Not country. Not polka. Carols."

The speaker responded with a cheerful polka version of **Deck the Halls**.

Finn glared. "Close enough," he muttered, jabbing at the buttons again.

Hannah swept in with trays of cookies labeled *Normal, Not Tampered,* and *Probably Fine.* Nobody laughed as loudly as she'd hoped.

"It's called humor," she muttered when people chose cookies strictly from the *Normal* tray.

Matt arrived ten minutes later, looking like a man fulfilling a contractual obligation. Snow dusted his peacoat, his jaw was set in detective-mode patience, and his eyes swept the room as though bracing for impact.

"Detective Hale!" Barb cried, clapping her hands. "You came!"

"Community relations," he said flatly, shooting me a look that translated to: *Don't gloat. Not even a little.*

"That's perfect," I said sweetly, handing him a cup of cider. "You can be my Bunco partner."

"Terrific," he replied in a tone that could've curdled eggnog.

Barb clapped again. "Ladies and gentlemen, roll those dice! And remember: every Bunco win brings us one step closer to unmasking the saboteur!"

"Pretty sure that's not how Bunco works," Finn murmured.

Dice clattered across tabletops like hail on a tin roof. The first round should have been simple—roll, tally, pass the cup—but this was Bunco in Marigold Lake, which meant chaos was mandatory.

"Snake eyes!" Marjorie Spence shrieked, though we weren't even on twos.

"That doesn't count," her partner argued.

"Counts in Vegas!" Marjorie insisted.

"We're in Iowa," her partner deadpanned.

At my table, Mrs. Holloway accused Mr. Peterson of palming a die, and he nearly flipped the table defending his honor.

"I have never cheated at a community event!" he cried.

"That's what a cheater *would* say," Mrs. Holloway retorted, adjusting her flashing brooch.

Sadie darted underfoot, chasing rogue dice with the determination of a seasoned security officer.

Matt, roped into rolling at the head table, tossed a pair of threes that clattered off the table and landed in the crockpot of meatballs.

The room erupted in shrieks.

"Beginner's luck," Barb said smugly.

Matt fished the dice out with tongs, jaw tight. "Remind me why I came again?"

"Community relations," I whispered back, biting my lip to hide a grin.

The game roared on—dice rolling, women shrieking "Bunco!" like they were summoning spirits. Barb narrated every roll like she was calling a horse race. Hannah refilled mugs. Finn was drafted as scorekeeper, though his attention wandered each time the speaker switched itself to polka again.

At my table, Marjorie leaned closer, eyes wide. "Did you hear? The choir director quit. Said she got a phone call telling her to keep her singers away from the Hometown Christmas."

A collective gasp rippled across the room.

"A call?" I asked.

"Anonymous," Marjorie confirmed. "The voice was disguised. Like someone talking through a kazoo."

Barb nearly snapped her pencil from excitement. "A kazoo criminal. Write that down, Claire!"

"I am not writing down 'kazoo criminal.'"

"Then I will," Barb said, scribbling furiously.

Across the room, Doris Temple leaned in conspiratorially. "Forget kazoos. My nephew says Maple Valley hired a professional sabotage squad."

"A what?" I asked incredulously.

"Like mercenaries," Doris said solemnly. "Only cheaper. And festive."

"You're thinking of mall Santas," someone muttered.

"No," Doris said gravely. "Sabotage squad. I read about them online. They wear matching scarves."

Barb scribbled:

Possible scarf mafia???

Meanwhile, Mrs. Holloway declared the whole mess alien-related. "Lights going out, stars disappearing—classic extraterrestrial activity. My cousin saw the same thing in Roswell."

Matt pinched the bridge of his nose like he was developing a headache large enough to need its own zip code.

The theories snowballed.

"Santa's suit is gone!" someone shouted. "Jerry went to the community center to try it on, and all he found was an empty hanger."

85

"That's sacrilege," Barb declared. "Tampering with Santa is a federal offense in Marigold Lake."

"Could've been misplaced," Matt said carefully.

"Nobody misplaces Santa," Barb said.

"Jerry misplaced his shoes last week," someone pointed out.

"That was different," Barb snapped.

From the back, a guest yelled, "I saw hoofprints behind the school! Looked just like reindeer."

"Or deer-deer," someone else said.

"Don't ruin the magic," Barb warned.

Meanwhile, Hannah brought out another tin of cookies. Sadie trotted to her side, nose twitching, and barked sharply at the tin.

I flipped it open. Half the cookies were smashed flat—like someone had intentionally pressed a hand into them.

"Hannah…" I whispered.

Her face went pale. "They were fine when I packed them."

Another sabotage. Small, but deliberate.

I glanced at Matt, who was being interrogated about Maple Valley's alleged mafia ties by an old woman wearing an apron that read *Kiss the Cook or Else*. I decided not to bring him the cookie crisis yet. His night was already difficult enough.

By the final round, cider had spilled, dice had vanished under couches, and Barb had interrogated half the players mid-roll. Someone's sweater caught fire when it got too close to a candle centerpiece (quickly put out by Finn dumping his cider on it). Sadie was drunk on crumbs.

When someone knocked over the cider pitcher, drenching half the score sheets, Barb shrieked like it was blood at a crime scene.

"Evidence destroyed!" she wailed.

"It's just paper," Finn said, blotting at it with towels.

"Just paper?" Barb gasped. "That was *proof*!"

Matt handed her a fresh copy. "Here's your proof."

Barb narrowed her eyes but accepted it.

As the crowd thinned and cleanup began, I carried empty mugs to the sink. Matt followed, lowering his voice.

"You need to be careful, Claire. These little things—cookies, costumes, rumors—they're adding up. Whoever's behind it is escalating."

"I know," I admitted. "But you can't expect me to ignore it."

"I can expect you not to get caught in the middle," he said softly.

I looked at him over the rim of a mug. "I'll try."

He gave the slow blink of a man fluent in Claire-speak. "That's code for 'don't hold your breath.'"

"Detective, you're learning my dialect."

"Unfortunately," he said, rinsing a mug beside me, "I'm fluent already."

I bumped his shoulder. "You'd be bored without me."

"Bored," he said, drying the mug, "but alive."

"Semantics," I said.

Sadie padded up with a stolen pretzel, crunching it like a closing gavel.

And as I watched Barb circle possible suspects—including **Kazoo Voice**, **Scarf Mafia**, and **Elven Mercenaries**—I knew one thing for certain:

The saboteur was only getting warmed up.

Chapter Eight

Sweet Treats and Sour Notes

By the time I padded into the kitchen the next morning, the Morning Glory felt... wrong.

Not "someone broke in and rearranged the furniture" wrong. More like "the house is holding its breath," like the B&B itself sensed we were in the middle of a slow-moving Christmas disaster.

Sadie trotted at my heels, her red scarf bobbing like she'd appointed herself deputy baker. Normally she'd run straight for the treat jar. Today, she sniffed the air, sneezed, and looked personally offended.

Can't blame her. The kitchen didn't smell like cinnamon rolls or rising dough. It smelled salty. Bitter. Betrayed.

Hannah stood at the counter, shoulders stiff, hair frazzled, and determination radiating off her like heat from an oven. She was stirring a mixing bowl like it owed her money.

"Tell me I'm not crazy," she said, not looking up.

"Depends," I said softly. "Is this about the snowmen cookies again? Because they were only slightly volcanic."

"No." She shoved the bowl toward me. "Taste."

I dipped a finger into what should have been sweet holiday joy. Instead, a mouthful of salt exploded on my tongue. I coughed—Sadie jumped—and Hannah groaned.

"Oh no," I said.

"Oh yes," Hannah snapped. "Someone swapped my sugar again. The whole canister. That's five pounds of sugar. Five! Claire, this is sabotage."

Sadie sniffed the bowl, snorted dramatically, and walked away with the air of someone who refused to be implicated in such culinary failures.

I lifted the sugar canister. Heavy. Sparkly. Innocent-looking. I tasted a pinch—salt. My stomach dropped.

The back door creaked open, and in swept **Mavis Rigsby**, queen of uninvited commentary and cinnamon coffee cake. Her scarf trailed behind her like a festive serpent.

"What's all the hollering?" she asked, setting a shopping bag on the counter. "I could hear Hannah from three houses down."

Hannah threw up her hands. "Sabotage! Salt in the sugar! Again!"

Mavis peered into the bowl. "Well, that looks rougher than my third husband's Christmas sweater."

"That sweater was homemade," Hannah muttered.

"And it showed," Mavis said.

She pulled out a thermos and poured coffee for Hannah, who took it like medicine.

"It's ruined," Hannah whispered. "My cookies... the church bake sale... the scones... everything."

"That's not true," I said gently. "We'll fix this."

"Fix it?" Hannah repeated, eyes wild. "With what? Christmas spirit and a candy cane?"

Before I could reassure her, Finn stumbled in wearing a T-shirt that read TECH SUPPORT ELF and sporting a cowlick you could see from space.

His eyes widened as he sniffed the bowl. "Oof. That's saltier than Barb when she loses at Bunco."

Hannah groaned louder.

Right on cue, Barb burst into the kitchen wearing a scarf that could blind a snowman. She stopped dead.

"What happened now?" she demanded. "Why do you all look like someone canceled Christmas?"

"It's the sugar," Mavis said. "Turns out it's salt."

Barb gasped, clutching her notebook like a lifeline. "Classic escalation! This is sabotage at a gourmet level."

Hannah smacked her forehead. "I knew it. I've been targeted. Someone wants to ruin my cookies."

"Or someone has a weird sense of humor," Finn offered.

Barb glared at him. "Not helpful."

Before Hannah could collapse into full gingerbread meltdown, Matt appeared in the doorway, stamping snow off his boots. His peacoat was still dusted with flakes, his hair a little mussed, and he held a coffee cup like he needed ten more.

"Tell me this isn't sabotage," he said.

"It's sabotage," everyone said at once.

Matt sighed the kind of sigh usually reserved for taxes. "Okay. Let me see."

He took one look at the bowl, pinched a tiny bit between his fingers, and tasted it with the resigned air of a detective forced to lick evidence.

"Yep. Salt."

Hannah groaned into her coffee.

"We'll log it with the other reports," Matt said gently.

"Other reports?" I echoed.

Matt ticked them off. "Missing star. Missing Baby Jesus. Choir director receiving threats. Santa's suit gone. And now... salted sugar."

Sadie barked sharply, as if adding a final bullet point.

"Escalation," Barb said triumphantly, scribbling furiously.

"Or coincidence," Matt muttered.

I folded my arms. "Coincidence doesn't replace sugar with salt."

Finn nodded. "That's a committed level of petty."

"We need supplies," I said decisively. "Hannah can't bake with three sticks of butter and a tub of sadness."

"And I have a schedule," Hannah added, pulling out her planner with trembling hands. "Do you know how many cookies I'm supposed to make today?"

"Nobody wants to know," Finn said.

"We're going," I said. "Now."

The Grocery Store Gauntlet

Getting our little investigative party out the door was less like leaving a B&B and more like launching a covert operation.

Hannah grabbed her baking list.

Barb grabbed her magnifying glass.

Mavis grabbed her insulated coffee tote—"for emergencies."

Finn strapped on a multi-tool and flashlight.

Sadie took the passenger seat like she was lead detective.

The grocery store was pure seasonal chaos. The air smelled like cinnamon brooms and desperation.

Shoppers charged down aisles with the determination of snowplow operators.

"Flour first," Hannah said, marching like a general.

She found a stack of flour bags and nearly cried with relief. "We're saved."

"Temporarily," Finn said, loading four into the cart.

Barb cornered a teenage cashier. "Tell me everything about the missing deliveries. Who intercepted them? Maple Valley? A rogue reindeer? Speak, boy!"

The kid blinked. "Uh... I just stock gum."

"Suspicious," Barb murmured, writing vigorously.

Meanwhile, Sadie found an inflatable snowman and barked at it like she was protecting the town from imminent frosty doom. The snowman wobbled dangerously toward a stack of peppermint bark tins. I lunged and caught it.

"Saboteur!" Barb yelled.

"It's an inflatable snowman," I said.

"Sure. That's what they want you to think."

After loading up on butter, sugar, and backup sugar "just in case," we headed back to the B&B.

Clues on Camera

By the time we'd hauled everything inside, Hannah was already baking like her life depended on it. Finn zoomed to the computer to pull up the porch cam footage again.

"There," he said, pointing.

A hooded figure approached the front steps around 12:23 a.m. Stood. Paused. Then stepped out of view.

"Look at the left hand," I said.

The figure held a bag. Small. Grocery-sized.

Mavis leaned close. "That gait is familiar. Looks like a bum knee."

"Could be Hardware Pete," I said slowly.

"Could be Lorraine from bowling," Mavis countered.

"Could be Santa," Finn suggested, "but like... off-duty Santa."

Matt frowned. "Could be anyone."

"Could be the saboteur," Barb declared triumphantly.

Sadie barked once—sharp and decisive.

A Sour Note

Later that afternoon, Hannah finally pulled a tray of perfect gingerbread from the oven, the kitchen filling with the warm smell of restored hope.

But the mood didn't last.

The moment I stepped into the parlor, the room buzzed with whispers.

The Petersons argued over choir rumors. Doris insisted the aliens were escalating. Frank, the historian, scribbled notes titled **Folklore of Festive Aggression**.

Then Mrs. Miller approached me with a frown.
"I just walked past the community center," she said. "The choir director was packing up her sheet music. Said she got another call."

"Another one?" I whispered.

"Anonymous. Told her to skip the Christmas Eve performance. Said it would be... safer."

The air left my lungs.

Behind me, Sadie whined softly.

Barb raised her notebook like a manifesto. "The saboteur is tightening their grip."

Matt stepped beside me. "We'll handle it," he said quietly.

But as I looked around—at Hannah's trembling hands, Finn's worried eyes, Mavis's furrowed brow, Barb's frantic notes—I realized something:

The saboteur wasn't just messing with decorations anymore.
They were targeting Christmas itself.

And something about it felt personal.

Chapter Nine

The Case of the Cancelled Carolers

By Tuesday afternoon, the Morning Glory felt less like a cozy inn and more like the buzzing hub of a small-town newsroom during a full-blown scandal. Voices layered over one another, rumors darted down the hall like migrating birds, and every guest seemed to be delivering the exact same breaking headline: the Marigold Lake Carolers had pulled out of Hometown Christmas.

"Canceled?" Barb hissed across the dining room, brandishing the newspaper above her head like she was about to cross-examine it. "This isn't just disappointing — this is sabotage of the highest order. A musical mutiny!"

I scanned the bold headline:

CAROLERS WITHDRAW FROM HOMETOWN CHRISTMAS

"It says they're sick," I said, though even the newspaper's tone seemed hesitant, like it didn't buy its own story.

"Sick," Barb repeated, her lip curling. "I saw four of those singers at the grocery store last night buying candy canes in bulk. Not one of them sniffled, coughed, or hacked. They've been frightened off."

Sadie barked once from under my chair — a sharp little sound that could've meant *I agree* or *someone dropped crumbs and you're ignoring them.* With Sadie, those were the only two possibilities.

The front door swung open, letting in a gust of cold air and a drift of snowflakes. In swept Mavis Rigsby, wrapped in a plaid coat and hauling a shopping bag that clinked with suspicious metallic noises.

"Don't tell me I missed the good gossip," she said, stamping snow off her boots with the authority of a woman entering a courtroom.

"You missed the worst," Barb replied dramatically, thrusting the newspaper toward her. "The carolers have quit."

Mavis set her bag on the counter with a thump. "Quit? Absolutely not. You don't drop out of Christmas. That's like skipping mashed potatoes at Thanksgiving — indecent. Un-American. Possibly illegal."

The Millers, stationed at the window table orchestrating their ritual mid-afternoon oatmeal-and-opinion session, chimed in immediately.

"It's Maple Valley," Mrs. Miller declared with the gravitas of a political analyst.

"Teenagers," Mr. Peterson grumbled from the next table, crossing his arms. "Always teenagers. They lurk. They plot. They prank."

Mrs. Peterson sniffed. "Teenagers don't know a treble clef from a cowbell. No, this is organized."

Across the room, Doris Temple stirred her coffee with a grim expression. "Mark my words — aliens. You tamper with Christmas music, and the extraterrestrials will find you."

Barb rolled her eyes so forcefully I thought she might sprain something.

Hannah swept in from the kitchen with a tray of scones, her cheeks pink and her hair frizzing in stress-induced static. She set the tray down with more force than necessary. "It's worse than that."

"Oh good," Barb said theatrically. "Hit us with it."

"They didn't cancel because of illness," Hannah announced. "They canceled because their sheet music was vandalized."

A gasp rolled across the room like a gust of wind.

"Vandalized?" I echoed.

"Pages ripped out, lyrics scratched over with marker, whole carols replaced with blank sheets!" Hannah's voice shook. "The director said it felt like someone wanted to silence them completely."

Barb clutched her chest. "Silence the singers! First the star, then Baby Jesus, now the choir. We're witnessing the collapse of Christmas culture."

Finn appeared in the doorway with his laptop and a granola bar. "Or somebody just really hates 'The Little Drummer Boy.' Ever heard Uncle Fred after eggnog? Sounds like sabotage to me."

"Fred is not a standard of measurement," Hannah said sharply.

The front door swung open again. Matt stepped inside, brushing snow from his shoulders, wearing the exhausted expression of a detective who had reached his annual quota for holiday emergencies on December twelfth.

"It's true," he said. "The carolers filed a report this morning. Their binders were slashed, pages swapped, and the majority of the music was unusable. No sign of forced entry, so whoever did it likely had access."

"An inside job!" Barb declared, scribbling furiously in her notebook.

"Or sloppy shelving," Matt countered. "We're investigating."

"Investigating?" Barb repeated. "Detective, this is *war.*"

Matt stared at her with a flatness so perfect it could've pressed wrinkles out of linen.

I set the paper down. "So what happens if they won't perform?"

"Then," Matt said simply, "Hometown Christmas loses its main event."

A ripple of horror murmured through the guests. Even Sadie whined, pushing her nose into my leg.

Later that evening...

The church basement rehearsal room was usually cheerful — the peppermint tea table set up by the piano, folding chairs arranged in tidy rows, the faint echo of tenors warming up. Tonight, it felt like the aftermath of a battlefield. Sheet music lay strewn across tables. Half-ruined binders were stacked like casualties awaiting identification.

"Look at this," the choir director said, holding up a binder. Thick black marker slashed across *Silent Night,* leaving only faint shadows of the lyrics underneath. Someone had doodled a lopsided star in the corner, like signing their work.

"Half our music is ruined," she said. "We can't perform like this."

Before anyone could respond, Mavis marched to the front like she'd been waiting her entire adult life to rally a demoralized choir.

"Oh, please," she said loudly. "A little ink never stopped Christmas."

The director froze. "I'm sorry?"

"You heard me." Mavis plucked a hymnal off the nearest table, flipped it open, and began belting *Deck the Halls.* Her voice cracked spectacularly halfway through the first *fa la la,* but she forged ahead with the determination of a woman who had survived three husbands and two decades of church committees.

Sadie barked in rhythm, tail wagging in enthusiastic support.

A few carolers snorted into their sleeves. One alto clapped politely.

"See?" Mavis announced proudly. "No vandal can silence Christmas."

"That wasn't exactly *inspiring*," Barb muttered.

"Neither is your kazoo theory," Mavis shot back.

The choir director exhaled slowly. "We... could do a shorter set. Maybe."

Barb gasped. "A shortened Christmas? What's next, unscented pine? Low-sugar fudge?"

"Barb," I whispered.

Matt crouched near the pile of binders, examining the pages with gloved hands. "No sign these left the building. No smudges except marker. Whoever did this probably slipped in during rehearsal or hid until everyone left."

"A choir infiltrator!" Barb announced.

"Or a jerk with a Sharpie," Finn said, taking photos.

I wandered toward a stack of hymnals. Sadie nudged her nose into the pile, sniffing like a tiny bloodhound. She pawed insistently at the stack, and when I moved it aside, a wadded sheet of paper fell out.

Another ruined page — but different.

This one wasn't just slashed. It was covered in doodles. Stick figures with X's for eyes. Jagged trees. A crooked star that looked eerily familiar, but I couldn't place why.

A chill tickled my spine.

"Matt," I murmured, handing him the page.

He studied it with a dark frown. "Not exactly adult hand-writing."

"Kids?" Hannah whispered.

"Maybe," Matt allowed. "Or someone trying to *look* like a kid."

Barb leaned close, squinting. "Three X-eyes means three conspirators. Obviously."

"No," Matt said flatly. "It doesn't."

But I couldn't shake the feeling that the crooked star meant something.

Back at the Morning Glory...

By the time we returned, the guests had gathered in the parlor like jurors awaiting a verdict.

"I heard Maple Valley hired a rival choir," Mrs. Miller whispered dramatically.

"I heard the vandal used red ink," Mr. Peterson said grim-ly. "Like blood."

"Aliens," Doris Temple insisted, pointing at the ceiling. "Music draws extraterrestrials. Ask Roswell."

"Oh, for heaven's sake," Mavis muttered. "If this were aliens, Doris, they'd have beamed up half the choir."

Barb marched to the center of the room wearing her Bunco-night scarf like a superhero cape. "Ladies and gentlemen," she began, striking a pose, "fear not! We will not let our town be silenced. The saboteur escalates — and so shall we!"

"Escalates?" Finn muttered. "This isn't World War III — it's sheet music."

"World War III started with less," Barb snapped.

The front door opened with a swirl of icy wind. Matt stepped inside, dusted with fresh snow, and held up a clear evidence bag. Inside: a ruined page of *Silent Night*.

"The bad news," he said, "is that the carolers won't be performing. They're too shaken."

A collective groan erupted.

"The good news," Matt added, lifting the bag, "is that the vandal left fingerprints. They're being analyzed now."

Barb shrieked, "Fingerprints! Civilization saved!"

"Let's not get ahead of ourselves," Matt said dryly.

He turned to me, his expression softening. Concern flickered in his eyes. "Claire... whoever's doing this is getting bolder. Targeting traditions. Community spaces. Next time, it could be closer to home."

Sadie pressed against my leg, warm and steady, a low growl humming in her chest.

I swallowed. "We'll be careful."

Matt sighed. "That's Fisher-speak for absolutely not."

"Detective," I said quietly, "you're learning my dialect."

"Unfortunately," he muttered.

Outside, snow drifted against the windows. Inside, the absence of carols settled into the room like a missing heartbeat.

The silence felt wrong — too sharp, too heavy.

And somewhere in that silence, the saboteur was smiling.

Chapter Ten

A Visit to Maple Valley

The drive to Maple Valley was short, but listening to Barb narrate every bump in the road made it feel like a cross-country trek.

The road curved lazily through fields glazed in white, the kind of winter postcard scene tourists loved and locals tolerated. Frost clung to the edges of the windshield, catching the morning light in tiny prisms that danced across the glass. From the passenger seat, Sadie alternated between watching the scenery and eyeing the bag of snacks at my feet like she was planning a heist. Hannah had insisted we bring granola bars "for morale," though Sadie clearly believed they were for her personal consumption. Every time the car hit even the smallest patch of uneven pavement, Barb made a noise as though we'd narrowly avoided plunging off a cliff. Finn, crammed behind me, muttered something about his spine realigning itself with each bump, while the smell of peppermint cocoa—Matt's compromise between coffee and holiday cheer—drifted through the SUV in warm waves.

"There!" she cried as we crested a hill. "Look at those tacky inflatables. Proof of a guilty conscience."

Her finger shot forward like we were spotting fugitives on the run. A yard below was peppered with blow-up decorations—snowmen, Santa, a neon penguin wearing sunglasses. If animatronics counted as residents, the house had a full census.

"They're snowmen," Matt said, eyes steady on the road.

His voice carried that detective monotone that suggested he was deeply regretting volunteering to drive.

"Exactly," Barb huffed. "Who puts seven snowmen on one lawn? That's hiding something."

I bit back a laugh. The woman could turn a minor holiday décor choice into a dossier-worthy crime. Finn leaned sideways, trying to get a better look through the frosted window while Sadie pressed her nose so close she left prints shaped like little comic-book speech bubbles.

The further we drove, the clearer it became Maple Valley had gone all-in on quantity over quality. One house boasted three competing nativity scenes—plastic, inflatable, and plywood cutouts—like the Wise Men were racing for property rights. A hardware store had lights strung so chaotically the sign read "SALE ON HORS _S" instead of "HORSE SALT."

The chaos grew funnier with each block. Maple Valley looked like someone had shaken a snow globe filled with tinsel and left it to settle in the wrong order. Children in oversized coats dragged sleds up a small hill near a church, shrieking with the kind of joy only found in cold fingertips and impending hot chocolate. A group of teenagers clustered around a small speaker, dancing poorly in heavy boots to a slightly off-key rendition of "Jingle Bell Rock." The scent of kettle corn drifted from somewhere nearby, warm and buttery despite the sharp wind. Still, under all the decoration, something felt... deflated. Like the town had put on too much glitter to hide a bruise.

Sadie pressed her paws to the window, growling at an inflatable reindeer that swayed ominously in the breeze. When it tipped forward, she yipped and scrambled into my lap as if begging me to sound the alarm.

Her whole body trembled with indignation, and I instinctively wrapped my arms around her, laughing quietly. The reindeer bobbed back upright, but Sadie glared at it as if daring it to fall again.

"See?" Barb whispered. "Even the dog senses villainy."

Sadie puffed out her chest in agreement. Or because she saw the doughnut sign again.

Or maybe she just didn't trust giant vinyl animals.

Honestly, I couldn't blame her. They had big unpredictable energy.

From the back seat, Hannah sipped from her thermos. "Maybe they just like snowmen."

She sounded tired, her voice hoarse from baking and stress. The poor girl hadn't had a single normal morning since the sabotage started.

Finn leaned over her shoulder, scrolling his phone. "Internet says Maple Valley once tried to break the world record for most inflatables in a parade. Disqualified for using duplicates."

He showed us an article headline with pride, as if this fun fact was a crucial piece of the investigation.

"See?" Barb said triumphantly. "Criminal masterminds."

Barb scribbled *Inflatable laundering??* into her notebook with a flourish.

Sadie yipped again, though it was probably more about the doughnut shop we passed on the corner than international scandal.

Her priorities were nothing if not consistent.

Main Street shimmered with lights, wreaths hung from lampposts, and a towering Christmas tree dominated the square. If I hadn't known better, I'd have thought Maple Valley's holiday spirit was untouchable. But closer inspection told a different story.

Shops that normally boasted cheerful window displays looked hastily thrown together, like someone had assembled them while running out the door. A cracked plastic snowflake dangled crookedly over a bakery window, spinning lazily in the breeze. A trash can overflowed with discarded cocoa cups, the snow around it stained brown. Voices carried across the square—frazzled, stressed, strained rather than festive. Somewhere, a choir track played through crackly speakers, slightly slowed, making "Joy to the World" sound like a dirge.

The tree's lights flickered unevenly, like a bad disco. Half the wreaths sagged. And on the town hall steps, two volunteers were locked in a heated argument while trying to reattach a crooked star.

Their dispute echoed across the square. Something about "wrong-sized screws" and "Sabotage, I swear it, Linda!"

"See?" I whispered to Matt. "Doesn't look like a town pulling off sabotage with military precision."

He exhaled softly, the breath fogging in the cold.

He shot me a sidelong look. "Don't let Barb hear you say that."

Too late.

Too late. Barb was already scribbling in her notebook. "Classic diversion technique. They ruin their own decorations to throw us off the trail."

I imagined Barb as a military general briefing troops on Operation Christmas Truth. Honestly? I could picture it too easily.

We parked near the square. Sadie bounded toward the tree, barking at the flickering lights.

Her paws sank into fresh snow with each proud step. She paused beneath the tree, nose lifting as though searching for clues among pine needles and faulty wiring.

A frazzled woman in a red parka intercepted us. "Careful, dog!" she warned, then sighed. "Sorry. It's been one of those weeks."

Her hair was tucked in a messy bun that looked like it had surrendered hours ago. Smudges of glitter clung to her cheeks.

Matt showed his badge. "Detective Hale, Marigold Lake. We heard your carolers cancelled too?"

The woman's relief was immediate. Someone else who understood the madness.

The woman groaned. "Cancelled? Sabotaged. Someone replaced their sheet music with blank pages right before rehearsal."

Her voice cracked with equal parts exhaustion and outrage.

Barb gasped. "The same tactic!"

She looked thrilled enough to levitate.

"Sharpie?" I guessed.

Please, let it at least be consistent sabotage.

"Glue," the woman said darkly. "Every note glued shut."

Barb scribbled *industrial sabotage??* in her notebook.

Hannah winced. "That's... creative."

And deeply annoying. Any baker could relate.

"And yesterday," the woman added, "someone poured glitter into the hot cocoa urn. The mayor nearly choked on sparkles."

Finn murmured, "A festive homicide attempt."

We decided to divide and conquer.

Barb barked orders like a general, and we scattered.

Finn trailed the extension cords like a detective at an electrical crime scene. He yelped once and muttered something about "suspects with bad wiring."

He'd insisted on bringing a multimeter, "just in case," which he now wielded with unnecessary dramatic flair.

A cluster of Maple Valley kids gathered around Sadie, giggling as she performed her patented sit-spin on the courthouse steps. One boy solemnly offered her a gumdrop, which she tried to swallow wrapper and all until I swooped in.

She stared up at me afterward, betrayed but chewing.

"Sorry," I said. "She thinks she's part goat."

A girl with pigtails nodded seriously. "My grandma says goats are excellent judges of character."

"Part hero," the boy corrected. "She barked at the tree when the lights flickered. That means she's on our side."

The kids nodded in solemn agreement, appointing Sadie their mascot.

Barb sniffed. "Obviously. Dogs can always tell who the saboteur is. I read it in a magazine."

"Barb's Home Investigations Weekly," probably.

Hannah returned from the bakery with a gingerbread man and a wary look.

The gingerbread man's expression mirrored hers.

"Well?" I asked.

She hesitated, which was answer enough.

She broke off a piece like a judge on a cooking show. "It's edible, but not Marigold Lake quality."

Barb gasped like this was the real crime.

"High praise," Finn said dryly.

His multimeter beeped at that moment, adding to the ambiance.

Hannah lowered her voice. "The baker was jumpy. When I complimented the spice, she muttered she was too distracted to measure straight. Then she whispered they'd had a 'strange customer' last week—asking way too many questions about festival setup. Not normal bakery talk."

My stomach tightened. That was definitely not normal bakery talk.

"Suspicious," Barb declared.

She wrote *Bakery spy??* with underlines.

"Or just nosy," Hannah countered, though her brow stayed furrowed.

Nosy was common. Sabotage? Not so much.

Meanwhile, Barb cornered a young choir member and interrogated him about budgets, candy-cane bribes, and costume receipts until the poor boy looked ready to defect to another holiday.

His eyes darted toward a nearby Santa display as though weighing escape routes.

"Sabotage by crafts," Finn muttered. "That's next level."

He snapped a picture of a frayed extension cord like it was evidence.

Near the tree, I met a man in a heavy coat, about sixty, with kind eyes and a weary smile.

His breath puffed out in slow clouds.

"Not our finest year," he admitted.

I appreciated the understatement.

"Problems here too?" I asked.

He nodded, jaw tightening.

He nodded. "Every time we fix one thing, something else goes wrong. Lights cut out, singers spooked, cocoa ruined. It's like someone's determined to steal the season."

He rubbed at his temple like the season itself had become a headache.

"Any idea who?"

I kept my voice low.

"Not Maple Valley. Not Marigold Lake either." His voice lowered. "Feels bigger. Like somebody outside wants to stir us up."

The idea sank into me with a cold weight.

He rubbed his gloved hands together. "My hardware store's been hit too. A whole order of outdoor paint went missing. And two boxes of extension cords."

Paint, cords, glue. Someone collecting supplies.

"That's not kids fooling around," I said.

Not unless the kids were running a black-market craft cartel.

"Exactly. Whoever it is knows what they're doing. And they're hoping we'll keep pointing fingers at each other."

He stared out at the flickering tree, sadness creasing his face.

Barb swooped in, notebook ready. "And who exactly are you?"

She always did love a dramatic entrance.

"Frank Danner. I run the hardware store."

Barb inhaled sharply.

"Hardware... glue... sheet music sabotage. Aha!"

Her pencil scratched triumphantly.

"Barb," I hissed. "Not everyone with a glue gun is a suspect."

Frank chuckled warmly.

Frank chuckled. "She's feisty. But she's not wrong—whoever's behind this knows their way around supplies."

He tapped his temple meaningfully, making Barb swoon like a detective fangirl.

Matt rejoined us, expression grim. "Officials confirmed: Maple Valley's Christmas is falling apart too. Which means your theory, Barb, is off the table."

Barb froze mid-scribble.

Barb gasped. "Off the table? But I already drew a diagram!"

She held up the notebook like sacred scripture.

"Erase it," Matt said.

He didn't even blink.

She clutched her notebook like a wounded animal.

The drama was palpable.

We regrouped at a café on the corner. Hannah bought muffins, Finn tinkered with the Wi-Fi until she kicked him under the table, and Barb lectured anyone within earshot about cross-town conspiracies.

The café was warm and smelled of cinnamon and new gossip. Snow dusted the windows, making everything feel enclosed, like a secret huddle.

Matt leaned close. "Heard anything useful?"

His voice was low, warm, just for me.

"Hardware Frank thinks it's someone outside."

I watched his eyes sharpen.

Matt nodded slowly. "Makes sense. I'll start a list."

He pulled a tiny notebook from his pocket, the kind real detectives used and Barb pretended to.

Barb leaned in. "Don't bother. I've already narrowed it down to six prime suspects, three secondaries, two maybes, and the aliens Doris mentioned."

Finn nearly choked on his muffin.

Finn smirked. "Add Maple Valley's Wi-Fi. If sabotage doesn't kill their Christmas, slow internet will."

He pointed toward the router, blinking in distress.

Hannah broke her muffin in half. "Say what you want, their bakery's better than their bandwidth."

Her loyalty to baked goods was admirable.

Barb ignored them, scribbling on a fresh page. "I'll call this the Saboteur Manifesto. Future historians will thank me."

She added a doodle of a magnifying glass.

"Future historians will burn it," Matt muttered.

I laughed into my cocoa.

I hid a smile behind my cocoa. For once, Matt wasn't defending Maple Valley. He was just as suspicious as the rest of us—only more careful about admitting it. In that moment, I knew we were finally on the same sleuthing page.

Caught between chaos and cinnamon steam, something warm fluttered under my ribs.

Sadie hopped into my lap, her paws dusted with muffin crumbs. She licked my cheek, and I whispered into her silky ear: "Looks like we're not chasing Maple Valley anymore."

Sadie stared up at me with bright eyes, ears perked like she knew exactly what I meant.

Her little nub tail thumped, as if to say the mystery had only just gotten juicier.

She gave Matt a pointed look, too, as if telling him to keep up.

Barb drafted her "Saboteur Manifesto," Finn argued with Hannah about cinnamon versus nutmeg, and Matt leaned close, his voice meant only for me.

The café hummed around us, warm and alive.

"You know you're going to poke your nose into this no matter what I say."

His tone was resigned but soft.

I smiled into my cocoa. "Of course. It's Christmas sabotage. Practically a civic duty."

He exhaled a laugh, small and reluctant.

He shook his head, eyes softening. "Just... be careful, Claire."

The warmth in his voice settled over me like a blanket.

Sadie sighed at our feet, as if she'd heard it all before and was already bracing for the next round of trouble.

And honestly? She probably was.

Chapter Eleven

Hidden Motive and Holiday Humbug

By the time we returned from Maple Valley, the Morning Glory parlor looked more like mission control than a cozy inn. Guests clustered around the fireplace, buzzing with theories as if they'd all been deputized overnight.

Snow still clung to our boots as we stepped inside, melting instantly on the warm wood floors. The smell of cinnamon, pine, and just a hint of burnt sugar—Hannah's emotional state manifesting in pastry form—hung thick in the air. The lamp near the fireplace cast a glow on half-finished cocoa mugs resting on coasters, abandoned like evidence in a makeshift detective lab. Even the usually serene quilt on the back of the sofa drooped crookedly, as though overwhelmed by the pressure of hosting so many amateur sleuths. Sadie strutted in with her chest puffed, energized by the collective drama, and immediately hopped onto her loveseat perch as if preparing to preside over the chaos.

"Mark my words," Barb announced, striding in like a general with her clipboard. "The saboteur isn't just after decorations. This is psychological warfare."

Her boots clicked sharply against the hardwood, each step a declaration of war. The clipboard—now thick with pages of her "Saboteur Manifesto"—rustled ominously as she waved it around like a weapon designed to intimidate both criminals and bystanders. Guests leaned in, eyes widening as though she'd just revealed an alien invasion plan. Somewhere behind her, Mavis muttered that Barb had watched too many crime shows. Sadie barked once, which Barb took as confirmation of her theory and not, as was more likely, a plea for someone to drop a muffin crumb.

Hannah appeared in the kitchen doorway, flour streaking her cheek. "It's also ruining my sugar cookies. Someone swapped my baking powder for cornstarch. Again."

Her apron was dusted in white like she'd face-planted into a snowdrift of pastry grief. The oven beeped behind her in a tone that could only be described as disappointed. For a baker like Hannah—whose emotional barometer was often measured by dough consistency—this was a full-scale crisis.

She held up a tray of flat, rubbery discs. Sadie sniffed one, wrinkled her nose, and backed away with the offended dignity of a queen rejecting an inferior tribute.

Even the guests recoiled a little, sympathetically wincing. The cookies sat on the tray like pale, deflated UFOs—culinary casualties of the saboteur's campaign. Hannah groaned softly, rubbing her forehead with the back of her hand, leaving a streak of flour like a stripe of battle paint.

"Even the dog refuses them," Hannah muttered.

Sadie huffed her agreement and repositioned herself by the fireplace, clearly distancing herself from the scene of the crime.

"Proof of tampering," Barb declared, scribbling furiously. "Chapter Four in my Saboteur Manifesto: Death by Dessert."

A few guests exchanged glances, torn between amusement and genuine alarm. Barb underlined her entry with fierce determination, as if preparing to send the cookies to a forensic lab. Meanwhile, Finn peeked over her shoulder, smirking as though contemplating submitting Barb's manifesto to an academic journal titled Conspiracy Studies & Cocoa-Based Crises.

"Barb," I warned, "don't terrify the guests."

One of the Millers, eavesdropping from behind a newspaper, nodded vigorously in support. Christmas sabotage was one thing—holiday-induced panic was another.

"They should be terrified!" Barb cried. "First our star, then our carolers, now Hannah's cookies. Christmas itself is under siege."

Her proclamation was dramatic enough to ruffle the garland on the mantel. A couple of guests gasped in unison, as though Barb had foretold the fall of civilization.

"Or," Finn said, strolling in with his laptop, "some people just can't bake."

He sauntered in like a man begging to get stabbed with a spatula. His laptop glowed with tabs—forums, emails, security footage—but his smirk said he was prioritizing sibling-style mischief over actual detective work.

Hannah hurled a cookie at him. It bounced off his shoulder with a dull thud.

The sound alone confirmed its viability as a projectile weapon. Guests chuckled nervously. Finn rubbed his shoulder dramatically as if grievously wounded, even though the cookie had probably injured itself more on impact.

Finn smirked. "See? Weapons-grade."

Someone snorted into their cocoa. Even Matt's lips twitched slightly.

Matt arrived not long after, his expression grimmer than usual. He'd been at the station all morning, and the set of his jaw told me the news wasn't good.

He shook snow from his coat, looking like a man carrying the weight of a dozen gingerbread-related felonies. His scarf hung crookedly, suggesting he'd put it on while pacing or muttering to himself on the way over. Sadie perked up as he entered, wagging her nub tail as though sensing something big was coming.

"We pulled prints from the vandalized sheet music," he said, setting a file on the coffee table. "No matches in our system. Whoever did it hasn't been in trouble before—or they're careful enough not to get caught."

A collective murmur rippled through the room. The fire cracked loudly, as though reacting to the tension.

Barb leaned forward. "So it's either a criminal mastermind or a choir dropout with a clean record. Narrowing nicely."

She jotted down criminal virtuoso?? with a circle around it. Hannah groaned loudly enough for half the room to nod sympathetically.

Matt ignored her. "But we do have leads. Two of them."

Every head turned toward him like synchronized holiday décor. Even Sadie sat up straighter.

The room hushed.

For a second, all that could be heard was the ticking of the mantel clock and the low hum of curiosity.

"First," he continued, "Grace Holloway's gift shop is struggling. If Hometown Christmas collapses, people might spend their money elsewhere—maybe at her clearance tables. She also has access to supplies like glue and craft paper."

The statement hung in the air like fog. Grace, the sweet woman who crocheted angels for fundraisers, now framed as a suspect? Even I felt the sting of that twist.

"Grace?" Hannah gasped. "She wouldn't ruin Christmas. She's the one who hand-painted those Santa mugs for the craft fair."

Her disbelief was so genuine it softened the room's tension. A couple of guests murmured in agreement.

"Desperation makes people do strange things," Matt said.

His tone wasn't accusatory—just pragmatic. Still, the implication settled uneasily in my chest.

"And the second?" I asked.

My voice came out quieter than I expected.

"Oliver Trent," Matt said. "New in town, renting a room above the diner. Claims he's here for 'small-town charm,' but folks say he's been asking a lot of questions about festival schedules, security... even electrical wiring."

A ripple of discomfort passed through the room. Trust in strangers dwindles fast in small towns.

Barb slapped the arm of her chair. "Sabotage by stranger! Classic humbug."

Her drama caused Mavis to snort in amusement.

"Or he's just lonely," Hannah said softly.

The room quieted, briefly human again.

"Lonely men don't care about outlet placement," Barb shot back.

Finn nodded solemnly, as if Barb's logic was unassailable.

Finn cleared his throat. "Speaking of outlets—look at this." He turned his laptop toward us, revealing a community forum. Anonymous posts filled the screen:

Waste of money. Cancel Hometown Christmas before someone gets hurt.

Marigold Lake couldn't organize a fruitcake sale, much less a festival.

The posts scrolled by like taunts.

"They went up yesterday," Finn said. "Whoever posted them used a VPN. Username: BahHumbug42."

Barb slapped a hand to her heart like she'd been mortally offended.

Barb gasped. "Forty-two! The answer to everything! It's a code!"

A guest whispered, "What's she talking about?"
Another whispered back, "Never mind. Just nod."

"Or they just like Douglas Adams," Finn muttered.

His tone suggested he feared for the literacy rate of the conspiracy theories forming around him.

Still, the words tightened my chest. These weren't random complaints—they felt calculated. Someone wanted us rattled.

Later that afternoon, Hannah and I walked downtown under the pretense of shopping, Sadie trotting happily on her leash. Marigold Lake bustled with holiday energy, but the mood carried an edge—like people were holding their breath.

Wind whistled between the buildings, tugging at wreaths and scattering stray ribbons along the sidewalk. Shop windows glowed with offerings of comfort—scarves, cocoa mixes, novelty elf mugs—but there was an unmistakable stiffness in the way people walked, in the way they spoke. Conversations were shorter, glances sharper. Even the familiar smell of roasted chestnuts from the corner vendor seemed tinged with unease.

We stopped at Grace's gift shop. Bells jingled as we stepped inside, releasing the scent of cinnamon candles and pine. The shelves were crowded but dusty in places, the kind of clutter that whispered of slow sales.

A small radio played soft instrumental carols, but the melody felt hollow. The dim lighting cast long shadows over ceramic figurines and mismatched ornaments. Sadie's paws clicked across the linoleum as she sniffed at a basket of knitted coasters, her ears folding back at the surprising lack of attention the shop received.

Grace stood behind the counter, rearranging clearance ornaments with the precision of a woman trying to will customers into existence. Her smile wobbled when she saw us.

The fatigue behind her eyes was unmistakable. She smoothed her apron reflexively, as though bracing herself for judgment she hadn't earned.

"Business okay?" I asked gently.

Her shoulders drooped before she managed a polite nod.

She sighed. "It's been slow. Everyone's waiting to see if the festival happens. If it doesn't..." She trailed off, straightening a row of ceramic reindeer. "This shop may not last until New Year's."

The confession hit like a stone. Grace's shop had been a quiet staple of downtown for years; its absence would feel like a missing tooth in the town's smile.

Half the shelves still held last year's stock: snowman salt shakers in faded boxes, garland tangled like forgotten necklaces, and a clearance bin of Baby's First Christmas 2019 ornaments. A hand-painted Sale! sign leaned tiredly against the wall, its red letters chipped.

The stagnant merchandise told its own bleak story. Even Sadie seemed subdued, sensing the heaviness in the air.

Grace's smile cracked. "Every December, Maple Valley pulls some new gimmick. Fireworks. A giant cocoa bar. How am I supposed to compete?" She pressed a Santa mug into Hannah's hands a little too firmly, then caught herself. "I mean... bless them, of course."

Her bitterness slipped out just long enough for me to catch it—a flash of resentment tucked beneath layers of Midwestern politeness.

Her voice softened, but a sharp flash lingered in her eyes.

That flicker unsettled me more than anything she'd said aloud.

"These are beautiful," Hannah said. "Did you paint them yourself?"

Grace brightened just a little, her pride showing through the exhaustion.

Grace nodded. "Every one." Her voice shook. "Takes me hours, and what do I get? Customers wanting discounts. Maple Valley's been stealing foot traffic for years. And now this..." She stopped abruptly, color rushing to her cheeks. "Anyway. Can I wrap something for you?"

Her abrupt pivot was telling—there was more she wasn't saying. Even Sadie lifted her head, sensing the tension.

As she set the mug down, I noticed a streak of dried glue on her knuckles. Coincidence—or not?

My stomach tightened. In a town full of crafters, glue meant nothing. But in a town under sabotage? It meant possibility.

We left with a cinnamon candle Hannah insisted on buying. Outside, she whispered, "You don't really think Grace—?"

Her voice trembled between disbelief and fear.

"I don't know," I admitted. "But she's under pressure."

The wind picked up, sending pine needles swirling along the curb like confetti from a defeated parade.

We hadn't gone far when I spotted a man leaning against a lamppost across the street, watching the square with unnerving intensity. Mid-thirties, trim coat, neatly combed hair—too polished to be loitering.

He stood too still, too stiff—like a statue disguised as a tourist. His gaze tracked every movement in the square, calculating and cool.

"That's Oliver Trent," Hannah murmured.

Her grip on the candle bag tightened.

He caught us looking and smiled politely, but his eyes flicked from Sadie to the electrical cords lining the sidewalk. He scribbled something in a notebook before heading toward the diner.

His interest in the cords made my pulse spike. That wasn't normal tourist behavior. Sadie growled low, her hackles rising beneath her cheerful red scarf.

"Wait," Hannah whispered. Oliver had stopped to question a volunteer stringing garland.

We paused at the corner, listening.

"How long do these lights stay up? Who checks them at night? Any weak spots in the wiring?"

His voice was smooth, confident—too confident.

The volunteer looked baffled, muttering something about "just plugs into the outlet." Oliver nodded briskly, jotting notes like he was auditing Fort Knox.

The volunteer backed away slowly, clearly unsettled.

Then he noticed us watching. His smile stayed polite but didn't reach his eyes. "Merry Christmas," he said smoothly, tucking the notebook away before slipping inside the diner.

His departure felt like a retreat—not from us, but from being observed.

Barb bustled up, out of breath. "Did you hear him? Weak spots in the wiring! He's plotting a blackout!"

Her scarf fluttered behind her like an alarmed cardinal.

"Small-town charm?" I muttered. "More like casing the joint."

Hannah nodded, still pale.

Sadie growled low in her throat.

Her instincts were rarely wrong.

"Don't bother hiding, Mr. Trent!" Barb hollered. "I've got your number!"

A couple of diners inside turned to stare. Oliver didn't.

He didn't turn.

Which somehow made it worse.

Back at the B&B, Finn had his laptop set up like a war room.

Sticky notes dotted the table like intel markers. Extension cords, battery packs, and half a cinnamon roll surrounded him, creating a chaotic shrine to both sabotage and snacks.

"Pulled more posts from BahHumbug42. Listen to this: Marigold Lake's parade is a joke. Even Santa wouldn't show up. And this one: Your cocoa is so weak it should be called hot water."

Barb gasped like she'd witnessed a crime against humanity.

Barb clutched her chest. "Insults against cocoa? That's personal."

For Barb, cocoa was practically a religion.

"It's bait," I said. "Someone's trying to rattle us."

And based on the shifting energy in the room, it was working.

Matt walked in just in time to hear. He rubbed the back of his neck, weary. "Claire, speculation is dangerous. Grace, Oliver, some crank online—they're all suspects until we have evidence. Don't jump ahead."

His voice was steady, but worry flashed beneath it.

"Speculation is my specialty," I said.

Sadie gave an approving snort, as if endorsing my credentials.

He gave me the look—the one that said he'd bolt the inn's doors if it kept me out of trouble.

I recognized the look. I ignored it regularly.

"I'll keep my nose clean," I promised.

A lie. A polite lie. But a lie nonetheless.

Sadie snorted, unconvinced.

Her judgment was fair.

That evening, the parlor was packed. Doris Temple insisted the saboteur was alien. The Millers swore it was Maple Valley. Barb stood like a politician on campaign night, reading from her Manifesto.

The crowd buzzed with nervous laughter and heated theories. Garland rustled as guests gestured wildly. The Christmas tree lights blinked in what felt like nervous Morse code.

"Friends, the saboteur is among us. Maybe a shopkeeper. Maybe a wandering stranger. Maybe even a digital phantom. But I, Barbara Jean Simmons, will unmask them before Christmas Day."

She jabbed her finger dramatically at the room, receiving raucous applause from the Petersons.

She punctuated her promise by slamming one of Hannah's ruined sugar cookies onto the table. It wobbled ominously.

A hush fell. The cookie did not crack. The cookie was invincible.

"Evidence," she declared.

Doris nodded solemnly, as if the cookie had spoken.

Sadie sniffed it, sneezed, and retreated. The room broke into laughter, tension cracking like ice.

Her sneeze echoed like a gavel, restoring order.

Doris wagged her finger. "Laugh all you want, but I still say it's aliens. First the star goes missing, then voices silenced. Classic UFO behavior."

She held up her binoculars like she expected visitors from space any moment.

The Millers countered immediately. "Nonsense. This is politics. Someone's trying to ruin Marigold Lake's reputation so Maple Valley gets the tourism dollars."

The Petersons murmured agreement.

"Or," Mavis piped up from the rocking chair she'd claimed, "it's just someone with too much time and too much glitter. A real saboteur wouldn't waste good sugar on Hannah's baking."

She sipped her cocoa smugly.

"Excuse me?" Hannah shot back, hands on hips.

Even her apron bristled.

"Just saying," Mavis replied with a smirk. "Even sabotage has standards."

Laughter rippled through the room again.

The guests howled, and for a moment the parlor felt less like a crime briefing and more like a comedy club.

Sadie sprawled on the rug, basking in the glow of communal chaos.

I leaned back, letting the fire's glow warm my cheeks. Matt sat across from me, quiet, steady, suspicion etched in the set of his jaw. Grace's trembling hands. Oliver's notebook. BahHumbug42's barbed words.

The pieces swirled in my mind like snowflakes in a bad storm—beautiful, confusing, and impossible to catch.

Suddenly, the sabotage felt bigger than glitter in cocoa or ruined carols. It felt personal.

The thought lodged hard in my chest.

Matt caught my eye. His voice was low, meant only for me. "Claire, promise me you'll be careful. This isn't just mischief anymore."

His tone slipped under my skin, soft and serious.

I smiled into my cocoa. "Of course. It's Christmas sabotage. Practically a civic duty."

The cocoa hid my grin—but not my intent.

He shook his head, but his eyes softened. "You're going to do it anyway."

He knew me far too well.

"Absolutely," I whispered.

Because stopping wasn't in my nature.

Sadie sighed contentedly at my feet, as if she'd heard it all before and was bracing for the next round.

She wasn't wrong.

Chapter Twelve

Confrontation and Christmas Chaos

The next morning, Marigold Lake hummed with tension. The parlor at the Morning Glory was thick with chatter, and not even the smell of Hannah's cinnamon rolls could sweeten the mood. Every guest had an opinion about the sabotage, and Barb fanned the flames like a talk-show host on too much caffeine.

Though the sun had barely crested the rooftops, the inn already felt overstuffed with worry. Snowlight filtered through the windows in pale blue sheets, catching floating dust motes as though they were suspended in suspense of their own. The usually cheerful mantel garland drooped like it had given up on optimism. Even the grandfather clock seemed to tick louder—as if keeping time on chaos.

"Mark my words," she declared, standing in front of the fireplace with Sadie perched like a furry sidekick at her feet.

"By sundown we'll have our culprit. The clues are piling up like fruitcake at a church bazaar."

Barb's voice carried with theatrical gusto, prompting several guests to stop mid-sip of cocoa to listen more intently. Sadie sat impressively regal, her little nub tail giving the occasional authoritative thump on the rug as though endorsing Barb's statement. Someone in the back whispered, "She's on a roll today," like they were watching a political debate, not breakfast drama.

"Fruitcake doesn't pile up," Hannah said wearily, balancing a tray of rolls. "It gets regifted."

The tray trembled slightly in her hands—not from the weight, but from sheer exhaustion. Her apron bore flour handprints like war wounds, and her hair had surrendered to a lopsided bun. She looked like a woman who needed a nap, a hug, and perhaps a sabbatical.

"Exactly!" Barb snapped her notebook shut. "Evidence regifted to me."

She tucked her pen behind her ear like she was preparing for a press conference rather than morning gossip distribution. Several guests leaned back, both amused and afraid of becoming her next "source."

Before I could intervene, the front door opened and Grace Holloway breezed in, more frazzled than festive—hair slipping from its clip, scarf half-untied. She set a box of hand-painted ornaments on the side table, looking like she was carrying the weight of every slow sale she'd ever had.

Cold air swirled in behind her, scattering pine needles from the wreath on the door. Her cheeks were flushed from the wind—or perhaps from frustration—and her hands trembled as she smoothed her scarf. The ornaments clinked in their box like delicate accusations waiting to be unpacked.

"I hear people are pointing fingers," she said, her voice sharp enough to cut through the din.

A hush began to ripple through the parlor. Conversations faltered, cups lowered, and every pair of eyes found Grace like she was the cliffhanger in a soap opera episode.

"Grace," I began.

Her name felt fragile on my tongue, but Grace spun toward me with the precision of a woman on edge.

She rounded on me. "Don't play innocent, Claire. Half the town thinks I'm behind this because my shop's struggling. You think I want Hometown Christmas to fail? It's the only time I make enough to cover January's rent."

Her voice cracked, just barely, but enough that even Barb paused mid-sentence. The raw honesty in her tone carried the weight of sleepless nights and dwindling sales. Hannah's eyes softened. Sadie edged closer, sensing tension.

Matt slipped in behind her, hands in his coat pockets, that calm he wore whenever a room needed cooling. "We just need to ask a few questions. Where were you the night the choir director got that call?"

The crowd leaned forward collectively, like spectators watching a tennis match that had suddenly become a courtroom drama. Matt's steady tone contrasted sharply with Grace's stormy energy.

Grace's face went tight. "At home. Painting ornaments. I didn't hear any phone calls."

Her hands fluttered for a moment before gripping the box again. The faint tremor of defensiveness radiated off her like static.

Barb gasped and scribbled. "Unverifiable alibi. Classic."

Someone snorted into their cocoa. Grace looked as though the notebook itself might be the next victim of a macramé-related assault.

Grace's shoulders sagged. She picked up an angel ornament, cradling it like proof of something fragile. "I stay up all night for these. My hands cramp. I sell one and it's like I've won the lottery. You don't think I'd sabotage the one thing that keeps me afloat?"

The angel in her hand caught the firelight, shimmering faintly as if begging the room to believe her. A murmur of sympathy stirred among the guests—until the glint of glue on her fingers sparked doubt once more.

As she lifted her sleeve, a scrap of dried glue caught the light. My stomach did an odd flip.

It wasn't incriminating by itself, but in today's climate, dried glue might as well have been a smoking gun.

"Grace," I said gently, "if you know something—"

A fragile stability teetered in the air.

"I know I'm tired of being accused." She grabbed the box and swept out, ornaments clinking like small broken promises.

The door banged shut behind her. Even the cinnamon-roll aroma paused, thickening in the silence she left behind.

The hush that followed was thin and brittle. Someone muttered about her rent going up; another whispered about "people changing after loss." Matt and I exchanged a look: desperation was a motive, not proof.

From the corner, Doris Temple made the sign of the cross with her spoon, dramatically whispering, "She's cracking." Mavis swatted her with a napkin.

He sighed. "She's not cleared."

His voice was low enough that only nearby guests heard—but of course that guaranteed the entire room would hear about it within minutes.

From his coat pocket, he pulled his phone. "And just so you know what we're up against—this came in from the choir director late last night."

Barb perked up like a meerkat with a megaphone.

He tapped the screen. A faint, tinny voice filled the parlor, warped by static. Keep the singers away. Cancel the carols. Or else Christmas won't be the only thing ruined.

The words bled into the room like cold water dripping down the spine. Several guests pressed hands to their mouths. Someone whispered, "Oh my stars." Sadie's growl deepened into a low warning rumble.

The voice was distorted—low, mechanical, like someone speaking through a broken kazoo. The room went utterly still. Even Sadie's ears pricked forward, a growl rumbling in her chest.

The distorted tone scraped at the nerves, its threat unmistakably personal. A log in the fireplace cracked sharply, making three people jump.

"Came through her landline," Matt said. "No caller ID. Audio's being analyzed, but so far—nothing."

His jaw ticked. Serious Matt was back—the one he used for real danger, not Bunco-night dramatics.

Barb clutched her scarf like a Victorian heroine. "Anonymous threats! Classic sabotage tactics. I've seen every Lifetime special on this exact thing."

She began listing titles under her breath—"Holiday Hostage," "A Christmas Conspiracy," "Tinsel Terror"—until Mavis shushed her.

Hannah's face paled. "So they're not just messing with decorations. They're scaring people."

The soft fear in her voice was enough to crack my own composure.

"Exactly," Matt said grimly. "This isn't pranks anymore. Whoever it is wants the whole town rattled."

A collective shiver rippled through the room.

That afternoon Hannah and I walked downtown with Sadie while Matt met with city officials. Volunteers were up ladders, stringing lights with mittened hands, but the cheer felt brittle. The canceled carols hung over the square like a cloud.

The wind carried faint strains of prerecorded holiday music, but even that seemed hesitant, as though the speakers themselves sensed danger. Kids tugged their parents along the sidewalk, but fewer smiles lit up their faces. Shop owners exchanged wary glances across the street, like everyone was waiting for the next shoe—or ornament—to drop.

That's when I saw Oliver Trent again.

He stood like someone frozen from the inside out—still, composed, too aware of his surroundings.

He stood by the lamppost outside the diner, notebook open, scarf tucked neatly at his throat. Too polished for a man supposedly chasing "small-town charm."

His gloved hand moved with precise strokes, making neat columns that caught the weak light. Sadie's ears flicked, picking up the subtle tension radiating from him.

"Look at him," Hannah murmured. "Sketching again."

We ducked behind a bakery stall, pretending to admire turnovers. Oliver jotted briskly, glancing at the cords running to the Christmas tree. Then he strolled up to a volunteer fussing with garland.

His movements were deliberate, like he was checking items off a list.

"How often do you test these outlets? Is anyone monitoring the square overnight? What's the backup if a strand fails?"

The volunteer blinked. "Uh... we plug them in and hope."

An uncomfortable laugh escaped her lips, but Oliver's expression didn't budge.

Oliver scribbled, glanced up—right at me.

For a moment, our eyes locked, and I felt like he was taking mental notes about me too.

"Planning the big event?" he called smoothly.

His voice was pleasant, but something cold flickered behind it.

"Funny," I said. "You seem more interested in how it falls apart."

He didn't flinch. Notebook shut, he disappeared into the diner. Through frosted glass I saw him at a booth, circling words: lighting, carols, parade route.

The circles were aggressive—almost accusatory.

"Who takes notes at a diner?" Hannah muttered.

"Someone planning a blackout," Barb whispered with relish.

She had seemingly appeared from nowhere, like a festive bat with impeccable timing.

The waitress leaned in; Oliver snapped the notebook shut so fast her tray rattled. When he noticed us watching, his smile was cool enough to chill cocoa. Sadie growled until the door closed behind him.

Sadie pressed against my leg as though pushing me away from invisible danger.

Barb puffed up, breathless. "Weak spots in the wiring! Practically a confession."

Her pen scratched like furious sleigh bells across her page.

"Or he's an engineer," Hannah said.

"Or a saboteur with a stationery addiction," Barb countered.

She pointed at Oliver's pocket where three pens peeked out like ominous antennae.

That evening, the town gathered for the Christmas tree lighting. Cocoa steamed in paper cups, carols played over the speakers, and kids craned their necks toward the giant evergreen glittering in the square. Frosty breath mingled with laughter.

But beneath the lights, a nervous energy pulsed. Parents kept a firmer grip on mittened hands. Volunteers stayed close to their equipment. Even the tree seemed to tremble faintly in the winter breeze.

Barb planted herself front-row, notebook poised. "Observe the saboteur in their natural habitat."

She whispered "saboteur" with the same reverence as one might say "rare bird."

"Barb," I hissed.

My warning was as effective as whispering to a blizzard.

The mayor took the microphone. "Welcome, friends, to Marigold Lake's annual—"

Before he could continue, a sound split the air—a groaning creak, deep and foreboding.

A collective gasp cut him off.

The towering tree shuddered. Slowly, like a felled giant, it tilted. Screams scattered the crowd. Cocoa arced through the air. A trombone let out a single, wildly off-key groan.

Chaos exploded like confetti in a hurricane.

The square dissolved into bedlam. Someone shouted the ropes had been cut; others rushed the bandstand, convinced the culprit lurked there. A trombonist clutched his instrument like he was ready to defect to a safer town.

Kids scrambled, parents grabbed, volunteers yelled conflicting orders. The mayor dove sideways, tripping over a candy-cane display. Frosted cookies flew like shrapnel.

Sadie barked herself hoarse, darting through toppled cocoa cups and runaway strollers. Hannah chased a tray of gingerbread men skittering across the snow.

It would have been funny if it weren't terrifying.

"Five-second rule!" Finn yelled, snatching one up to the collective horror of onlookers.

He shrugged while chewing. "Still good."

"Sabotage!" Barb crowed. "I told you so!"

She wrote furiously, nearly tearing through the page.

The tree crashed, scattering ornaments like frozen confetti. Shouts rippled through the crowd: the ropes had been sawed clean through.

Volunteers stared in horror at the severed fibers. The cuts were neat—too neat.

Matt tore forward with me at his heels. The frayed fibers were deliberate.

His eyes narrowed, assessing the damage like a surgeon examining a wound.

"They wanted this to happen in front of everyone," he said, jaw set.

The realization made my pulse throb.

"And it almost crushed the mayor," I whispered.

A volunteer nearby nodded, pale. "Half a foot to the left…"

Barb bustled up. "Attempted tree-slaughter! That's a felony in three states!"

Several heads whipped toward her, confused.

"Not a legal term, Barb," Matt barked.

He didn't even look at her—he knew better.

"Should be," she sniffed.

Her indignation steamed in the cold air.

Amid the chaos, Mavis barked orders like a seasoned sergeant. "Lift with your knees! Watch the kids! Somebody get a broom!" Her practicality was absurd and oddly comforting.

Her presence stabilized the moment more effectively than any official.

Parents huddled children close. Volunteers steadied the half-fallen evergreen. Hannah crouched by a shattered ornament, eyes glossy. "They've gone too far," she whispered.

The ornament in her hand reflected the ruined scene like a funhouse mirror.

Finn, already filming, muttered, "This'll be viral by morning. Great for awareness, terrible for nerves."

His camera caught everything—chaos, fear, broken lights, toppled tinsel.

Barb waved her arms like a frazzled MC until someone lobbed a marshmallow at her. It stuck to her cheek.

She froze, eyes wide, then swiped it off with dramatic disdain.

By the time the crowd thinned, the mayor—shaken but unhurt—was led away. The tree lay in ruin, ornaments crushed into the snow. Matt stood rigid, voice hard. "This is more than pranks. This is reckless endangerment."

His words cut through the remaining noise like icicles breaking.

Barb gasped. "Finally! A serious charge!"

She scribbled "felony???" with stars around it.

I hugged my coat tight, a chill settling deeper than the cold. For all the marshmallows and Mavis's orders, fear clung to the square like smoke.

The broken decorations, the crushed cocoa cups, the scattered footprints—it all felt like the aftermath of a warning.

Matt turned to me, eyes dark. "Stay out of this, Claire. Whoever's behind it doesn't care who gets hurt."

His voice trembled faintly, betraying fear.

I nodded, but the look we shared said otherwise.

We both knew I wouldn't stay out of anything.

Sadie leaned against my leg, warm and steady. She gave a small bark, as if closing the matter.

Her little body trembled with leftover adrenaline, but her eyes were sharp—watchful.

We trudged home through falling snow, the echo of the toppled tree following us like a warning.

The snow muffled the world around us, yet the silence felt louder than ever.

Chapter Thirteen

A Christmas Miracle

If Christmas spirit could be measured in sparks, Marigold Lake was dangerously close to burning out—and not just because someone had nearly flattened the mayor with a pine tree. The toppled evergreen still lay across the square like a fallen soldier, its ornaments shattered and its crown bare where the missing metal star should have gleamed. The air the next morning was heavy with worry, not cinnamon and cocoa the way December mornings were supposed to be.

Even stepping outside felt different. The normal December hush—the kind that made you think of hot cider and quiet snow—had been replaced by a prickly tension. People hurried in clusters rather than strolling; conversations were conducted in lowered voices, with frequent glances over shoulders. Even the holiday wreaths hung from lampposts seemed to droop with unease. Somewhere in the distance, a hammer echoed as volunteers attempted repairs, each strike a reminder of what had been broken.

Inside the Morning Glory, the parlor looked more like a war room than a cozy sitting area. Volunteers dropped in for hot drinks, whispered about suspects, and drifted back out to face the mess in town. Barb had declared herself "acting commissioner of spirit preservation" and was holding forth by the fireplace like a general addressing her troops.

She had even repositioned the armchairs to face her like she was hosting a tactical debriefing. Half-drunk cocoa cups littered the side tables. The usually gentle crackle of the fire was drowned out by the rising pitch of speculation. Sadie had stationed herself near the hearth like she was expecting to be promoted any moment.

"Listen up," she barked, notebook in hand, Sadie perched proudly at her feet like a furry second-in-command. "We are under siege. The saboteur wants us scattered, frightened, humiliated in front of Maple Valley. Well, not on my watch. Bunco ladies stand tall!"

A few guests exchanged looks that hovered somewhere between amusement and fear, but no one dared interrupt Barb mid-speech. Sadie, meanwhile, puffed up like she fully understood the gravity of her honorary rank.

Half a dozen women, still wearing sequined reindeer sweaters from the night before, saluted her with cinnamon rolls. Doris Temple clutched binoculars she'd borrowed from her son-in-law and announced she was covering "airspace in case of low-flying drones." Marjorie Spence had a walkie-talkie she didn't know how to use but insisted was "essential for neighborhood defense."

The walkie-talkie crackled occasionally, emitting bursts of static that made everyone twitchy. Doris kept adjusting the focus on her binoculars despite being indoors, announcing every time she saw something "ominously red"—which usually turned out to be a poinsettia.

Finn groaned from his corner, laptop balanced on his knees, wires sticking out like a mad scientist's lair. "She's not wrong about the sabotage, but can we cool it on the coup d'état speeches? My Wi-Fi can't handle this kind of stress."

His voice was half-drowned out by the whirring fan of his laptop, which had been running at full speed for hours. A tangle of chargers and USB cords snaked across the floor like holiday tinsel gone rogue. Sadie eyed the cords warily, as if she suspected sabotage could happen there too.

"What are you even doing?" I asked, peering over his shoulder.

"Cross-checking the square's security footage with the power grid logs," he said without looking up. "Whoever cut the tree ropes also tampered with the outlets. Look—" He pointed at a pixelated frame where a dark blur hovered near the cords an hour before the collapse. "See that shadow? Too tall to be a kid, too quick to be a raccoon. Someone knew where to cut power without frying themselves."

The image flickered again, and a ripple of unease ran through me. Sabotage was one thing—deliberate danger was another. Even the room seemed to go quieter, guests leaning in as though they might see the culprit materialize from pixels.

"Can you clean up the image?" Matt asked, arms folded as he leaned in the doorway. His tone was steady, but his jaw had that detective-set tension I'd come to know.

The way he stood—broad shoulders blocking the draft from the hallway, boots still dusted with snow—told me he'd come straight from the square. He smelled faintly of cold air and pine. Even though he tried to sound calm, worry clung to him like frost.

Finn tapped a key and the blur sharpened just enough to suggest a figure. The coat looked familiar—neatly buttoned, collar popped, scarf tucked just so.

Oliver Trent.

I felt my stomach dip. "Of course."

That sinking feeling spread like icy water down my spine. I replayed Oliver's peculiar questions, his habit of lurking near electrical cords, his too-calm smile. It all clicked uncomfortably into place.

Barb gasped. "The stationery saboteur! I knew it. No one sketches that much without evil intent."

She slapped her notebook shut dramatically, nearly knocking over Marjorie's walkie-talkie, which responded with an indignant burst of static.

"It's not proof," Matt warned. "But it's enough to ask more questions."

His expression didn't soften. The responsibility of keeping the town safe weighed on him, and moments like this made it visible, like a dim bruise beneath the surface.

Hannah clattered in then, cheeks pink from the cold, carrying two baskets of rolls. "Questions later—help me pass these out. People need food before they declare mutiny."

The smell—warm sugar, toasted pecans, a hint of nutmeg—briefly loosened the tension in the room. A few volunteers perked up at the sight of the baskets, hands already reaching.

She shoved a basket into my arms and one into Matt's. We made rounds like makeshift morale officers. Guests and volunteers perked up as the smell of butter and sugar cut through the tension. Sadie darted ahead of me, nosing at mittens until people laughed and fed her a crumb or two.

Hannah's strategy was working; you couldn't panic fully while holding a warm bakery item. The mood brightened by degrees—the crackle of the fire became comforting again, conversations softened, shoulders relaxed.

"See?" Hannah said, hands on her hips. "Cookies first, panic later. It's the Marigold way."

Barb sniffed. "Cookies are a bandage. We need surveillance. A neighborhood watch. A civilian patrol!" She waved her notebook like a manifesto. "The Bunco ladies are ready for duty."

Several of the Bunco ladies straightened in their chairs, nodding so vigorously their antlers bobbed. One adjusted her sweater as though preparing for a covert mission involving tinsel.

The women murmured agreement, adjusting antler headbands with grim determination.

By late afternoon, the square looked patched together but not hopeless. Volunteers had propped the tree upright with heavy supports. Kids tied paper ornaments to replace the shattered glass ones. The choir director, still shaken from the threatening phone call, let two brave singers stand at the edge of the square with hymnals. Their voices quavered but carried through the chilly air.

Even the air smelled like resolve—a mix of hot cocoa from the nearby booth and pine sap from the damaged tree. People moved carefully, speaking in subdued tones, as though afraid to break whatever fragile momentum they'd regained.

I stood with Hannah, watching. "It's not perfect," she said, "but it's something."

Sadie sniffed at the base of the tree, nub tail twitching. She barked once, sharp.

I crouched beside her. "What is it, girl?"

Her ears were high, alert, tracking something beneath the layers of snow and footprints. The space felt charged, like the moment before a storm.

Matt joined us, scanning the ground. A coil of cut rope lay half-buried in the snow, the edges stained with something dark.

"Oil," he said grimly, touching it with his gloved fingers. "Fresh. Whoever cut this used a saw coated in lubricant."

The revelation hit me like a slap of cold wind. This wasn't the work of a clumsy prankster. Someone had come prepared—someone who knew tools, materials, timing.

Finn appeared, breath puffing clouds. "I cross-referenced power surges last night. Guess where the strongest one was? Right at the diner. Guess who was inside with a notebook?"

"Oliver Trent," I finished.

Barb came barreling up, scarf flapping like a victory banner. "And guess what I just heard? Someone spotted Oliver behind the bandstand last night. With a toolbox!"

She delivered this as though she'd solved the entire case and was ready for her commendation ceremony.

Matt held up a hand. "Slow down. We need facts, not gossip."

"Facts are gossip, just dressed for court."

Before Matt could argue, the mayor climbed onto the bandstand with a microphone. "Friends, despite setbacks, tonight we light this tree again as a sign that Marigold Lake will not be defeated."

Families pressed closer. Children hoisted onto shoulders. The air hummed with equal parts hope and anxiety.

Applause rose, hopeful but thin.

The switch was thrown. For a glorious heartbeat, the tree blazed gold from top to bottom—though its crown was bare where the stolen star should have gleamed. Children clapped mittened hands. Hannah squeezed my arm.

Then the lights sputtered. Flickered. And died.

The gasp that followed felt like the entire town inhaling in fear at once. Even the snowflakes seemed to hesitate midair.

Gasps swept the square. Darkness pressed in, broken only by the weak glow of a few lampposts. Somewhere in the crowd, a child cried.

"Blackout!" Barb shouted. "Classic sabotage!"

Sadie barked furiously, tugging at her leash toward the diner.

Matt swore under his breath. "They hit the grid. Stay here—"

"Not a chance," I said, already following him.

The crowd surged like a single creature, startled and disoriented. People stumbled toward the edges of the square, gripping coats and mittens, voices rising in confusion.

We barreled into the diner, Finn close behind. Oliver sat in his usual booth, notebook open, face lit by the glow of a battery lantern. Calm. Too calm.

The diner, normally warm and bustling, felt eerie in the emergency glow. Steam rose from abandoned mugs of coffee. A few patrons huddled near the windows, watching the darkened square with wide eyes.

Matt slammed a hand on the table. "Power's down in the square. What do you know about it?"

Oliver raised his brows, infuriatingly polite. "Detective, I'm merely documenting. Observing."

"Observing sabotage?" I snapped.

He tilted his head. "Is it sabotage—or just incompetence revealed under pressure?"

The room went still. Even the clink of dishes ceased. Oliver's voice was smooth, but there was something sharp beneath it—a practiced detachment that didn't match the rising fear outside.

Before Matt could reply, Finn shoved his laptop across the table. "Caught you. The diner's Wi-Fi router logged a spike at the exact second the lights cut out. And guess whose device shows up? Yours."

Oliver's calm cracked for the briefest moment—a muscle twitched in his jaw, his hand tightened on the notebook—but it was enough to set my heart racing.

Matt leaned closer, voice steel. "Stay seated. You're not going anywhere."

Oliver's smile was tight, not warm. "Careful, Detective. In small towns, it's easy to mistake curiosity for guilt."

"Funny," I said, "because in small towns we also know when someone doesn't belong."

Back in the square, panic softened to murmurs as Hannah and Mavis lit candles and passed them through the crowd. The glow spread, warm and golden, pushing back the dark. Children clutched cookies in one hand, candles in the other.

Voices rose, shaky but strong, until the square shimmered with flame and song.

The scene stirred something deep in my chest—a reminder that Christmas spirit wasn't something you could plug in or cut down. It lived in people, in community, in stubborn joy.

"It's not lights," Hannah called, voice steady, "but it's ours. And no saboteur gets to take that from us."

The crowd rallied. Even the choir director, voice trembling, lifted her head and joined.

Barb clutched her notebook like scripture. "A miracle," she whispered.

I glanced at Matt, who still had Oliver pinned with his stare. "Maybe not a miracle," I said softly. "But close enough."

Sadie barked once, her silhouette sharp in the candlelight. Her little nub tail wagged like she already knew: the saboteur wasn't done yet, but neither were we.

Chapter Fourteen

Candles, Cocoa and Close Calls

The square smelled of scorched pine and peppermint when I stepped out the following evening. Volunteers still bustled, but the frantic edge had eased into something steadier.

A thin veil of snow drifted over the rooftops, settling onto garland and storefront awnings like powdered sugar dusted by a giant baker. Music from a portable speaker warbled between songs, glitching every so often as if the holiday spirit itself were trying to catch its breath. People walked slower tonight—gentler, somehow—like they were consciously holding the town together with their presence.

Paper lanterns hung from the bandstand, and long tables sagged under pies, cookies, and at least four versions of hot chocolate—plain, peppermint, spiced, and something Doris Temple insisted had been "fortified against alien infiltration."

The lanterns bobbed with each gust of wind, casting moving halos across the snow. Kids darted between the tables, leaving trails of tiny boot prints. Even the inflatable snowman—hastily patched after deflating earlier—seemed to lean forward like it was listening for trouble. If sabotage was coming, the whole square looked ready to face it together.

"Mark my words," Barb said as we set out mugs, "if the saboteur shows up here, I will personally bean them with a gingerbread man."

She held one up as proof—dense, over-baked, and perfectly capable of concussing a grown man. Barb wielded it like a badge of office. Her scarf, a red-and-green monstrosity, flapped dramatically every time she gestured, adding accidental slapstick flair to her threats.

Sadie pranced between legs, sniffing at spilled marshmallows and barking whenever a lantern swayed too low.

She stopped every few seconds to glance back at me, as if making sure I understood she was taking her role as Deputy Holiday Security very seriously. A little boy dropped a gumdrop, and Sadie inhaled it whole before he even noticed. The boy clapped like she'd performed a magic trick.

Hannah held court at the cookie table, doling out sugar with the gravity of a general distributing rations. The Petersons quarreled over gingerbread texture. The Millers traded recipes like contraband.

The din of voices rose and fell like waves—arguments, laughter, gossip, the clink of mugs being refilled. Even bickering sounded warmer tonight. Someone tuned a violin near the choir, producing a wobbly series of notes that made a nearby toddler cover her ears. Across from them, volunteers rigged a makeshift windblock of quilts to protect the cocoa table from gusts.

For once, the hum of voices was stronger than the memory of fear.

It wrapped around us like an invisible shield—thin in places, yes, but real. People leaned in to retell the story of the falling tree with wild embellishment: "It missed the mayor by an inch!" "No, by a foot!" "No, he rolled out of the way like an action hero!" Even the ridiculous versions helped.

Then the lights flickered.

A split second—the kind that stretches—and the entire town seemed to inhale at once.

A gasp rippled through the crowd, but the glow steadied. A child squeaked, "Do it again!" and laughter scattered the tension. Still, I caught Matt's gaze across the square—his expression tight, cataloging every cord, every shadow.

Even from here I could see the tiny muscle ticking at his jaw—the one that only appeared during casework or when Barb said the words "community investigation." His eyes swept over rooftops, alleyways, and the edges of the square with the precision of a man expecting the worst but hoping desperately for the best.

We gathered near the bandstand as a small choir braved a few carols, their voices thin but steady.

The harmonies wobbled, but the crowd leaned in, bolstering them with humming, soft singing, and warm applause. The cold turned breaths into puffs of fog that floated around the singers like stage effects.

This time, when a lantern guttered out, half the crowd simply pulled candles from their coats as if they'd been planning it all along. Not desperate this time, but defiant.

A quiet murmur passed through the square—not panic, but something like pride. Children watched their parents light candles and mimicked the motion in earnest seriousness, as though participating in an ancient ritual.

Sadie pressed against my leg, eyes glinting in the candlelight. Barb leaned close, whispering like a spy novel narrator. "Notice how they wait until spirits are highest to strike. Classic villain timing."

Her breath puffed white in the air, mingling with candle smoke. She held her gingerbread weapon tighter, scanning the square with squinty-eyed suspicion that would've made any bystander feel guilty even if they'd done nothing more sinister than over-salt a casserole.

But no attack came. Just the flicker of candles, the steam of cocoa, and neighbors leaning close against the cold.

The absence of chaos felt almost eerie—like the quiet before snowfall or the moment between heartbeats when you're waiting for something to happen. Even the choir began sounding braver, their notes smoothing out into something steady and sweet.

Mavis appeared at my elbow, pressing a cookie into my hand. "Don't look so worried," she said. "They can knock down trees, cut ropes, and ruin sheet music. But they can't ruin this. Not unless we let them."

Her eyes softened with something fierce and grandmotherly, the kind of determination that could anchor a storm. The cookie she handed me was warm—fresh from one of her mysterious insulated tins—and smelled like molasses and stubbornness.

The choir began Silent Night, the notes fragile but true. Children sang with sticky mouths, couples swayed, and even the Petersons hushed. My throat tightened. For one fragile, perfect moment it felt like Christmas had won.

The candlelight reflected on faces around the square, painting everyone in soft gold. Snowflakes drifted lazily, catching the glow and turning it into glitter. Sadie let out a small sigh, her tail sweeping slowly across the snow.

Then I saw him.

It was only a flicker of movement at first—something too still in the sea of swaying bodies.

At the far edge of the square, half-hidden in shadow, a tall figure in a dark coat stood watching. Not singing. Not smiling. Just watching.

He leaned slightly forward, posture unnervingly attentive. For a heartbeat I thought I recognized the tilt of his head, the set of his shoulders—but the distance muddied certainty. The lanterns didn't reach him, but the faint glow of a storefront sign caught on the edge of his sleeve.

I blinked, and he was gone.

No crunch of footsteps. No retreating silhouette. Just empty snow settling where he had been.

Sadie barked once, sharp, ears pointed toward the dark.

Her entire body went rigid, alert in a way that made the hair on my arms rise. She pulled at her leash, not wildly, but with insistence—as if she knew something I didn't.

The song carried on, but my heart thudded with the reminder: the saboteur hadn't finished.

And somewhere beyond the warm spill of candlelight, the cold shadows waited.

Chapter Fifteen

Restoring the Spirit

The morning after the blackout, Marigold Lake looked like a town that had been through battle. The tree still leaned against its wooden braces, its crown bare where the missing star should have gleamed. Broken ornaments had been swept into boxes, cords coiled like snakes waiting for another strike.

And yet, something had shifted.

Instead of slumped shoulders and muttered suspicions, there was motion. Purpose. A steady hum of determination ran through the streets as volunteers hammered, swept, and carried supplies. Children marched down the sidewalks with paper chains longer than they were tall. The air smelled of pine, coffee, and sheer stubbornness.

At the Morning Glory, the parlor had once again transformed into command central. Barb presided at the fireplace, wrapped in a red sweater studded with sequins that spelled BELIEVE, her notebook balanced on her lap like scripture. Sadie sat at her feet, alert and smug, as if she'd been promoted to chief of staff.

"Citizens," Barb announced, "I have compiled a list of morale-restoring measures."

"Here we go," Finn muttered, hunched over his laptop at the corner table. Wires sprawled from his machine into a nearby outlet, which he eyed as though it might bite.

"Number one: increased surveillance," Barb continued. "Doris Temple is stationed by the post office, binoculars in hand. Marjorie Spence is monitoring suspicious packages at the grocery. And I, of course, am directing operations from here."

"You're just drinking cider and heckling people," Finn said.

"Leadership requires hydration," Barb sniffed.

"Hydration's water," Hannah called from the kitchen. "Not mulled cider and brandy."

A crash punctuated her words. I poked my head into the kitchen to find her standing in a dusting of flour, hair powdered like she'd walked through a snowstorm. Cookie sheets covered every surface, and the oven timer blared like an alarm.

"Everything okay?" I asked carefully.

"Fine," she said through gritted teeth. "Except the shipment of vanilla never came, so I substituted almond. And someone—" she glared at Finn through the doorway—"moved my nutmeg next to the cinnamon, and I grabbed the wrong one."

Finn didn't even look up. "If cinnamon sabotages you, that's on Maple Valley."

Hannah banged a pan onto the counter. "Don't joke. These cookies are the backbone of morale."

Sadie trotted in, nose twitching, and sat in front of the tray of lopsided gingerbread men with saintly patience. Hannah sighed, broke one in half, and handed it over.

"Great," she muttered. "Even the dog's judging me."

"Not judging," I said. "Supporting."

Sadie wagged her nub tail in agreement, crumbs dotting her whiskers.

By midmorning the B&B felt like a train station. Volunteers streamed in with boxes of paper chains, stacks of cookies, and armfuls of pine boughs. Guests lingered, offering hands where they could. Even the Petersons, bickering all the way, were spotted carrying wreaths together down Main Street.

Mavis arrived just after ten, bundled in a sensible coat and radiating efficiency. She strode into the parlor, clapped her hands, and declared, "Enough wallowing. We rebuild."

Barb blinked. "Excuse me, I'm already rebuilding morale through strategic oversight."

"Strategic oversight doesn't hammer nails," Mavis said briskly. She pointed at Finn. "You—find us another generator in case the grid goes again."

Finn raised a brow. "You know those cost money, right?"

"Then borrow one, steal one, or build one out of your wires. Just do it."

Finn actually looked intrigued.

"You—" Mavis turned to Hannah. "Feed these people. No one saves Christmas on an empty stomach."

Hannah bristled, then nodded, a spark of determination back in her eyes. "On it."

"And you—" Mavis faced Barb.

Barb squared her shoulders, braced for orders.

"—stay out of the way."

Barb gasped so loud Sadie barked in alarm. "Stay out of the way? I am the heart and soul of this investigation!"

"You're a distraction," Mavis replied calmly. "Take notes if you must, but don't block the workers."

Barb clutched her notebook like a wounded general. "This town will thank me someday."

"Maybe," Mavis said, already marching toward the square, "but not today."

I bit back a laugh and slipped my coat on. Matt was waiting by the door, his own coat buttoned against the cold. "Want to make rounds?" he asked.

We walked through town together, Sadie bounding ahead, paws kicking up snow. Everywhere we looked, neighbors worked: teenagers stringing lights, retirees painting plywood cutouts, shop owners sweeping broken glass from their storefronts. It wasn't polished—it was patchwork and messy—but it was progress.

Matt slowed near the tree, where children taped paper stars to the lower branches. "They're not scared," he said quietly.

"No," I agreed. "They're stubborn."

Snow dusted his dark hair. He looked down at me, and for once, duty hadn't hardened his expression—there was softness there. "You know this could've gone differently last night. If the tree had fallen faster..."

I shivered. "I know."

His hand brushed my arm, brief but steadying. "I just don't want you in the middle when it happens again."

"Too late," I said, forcing a smile. "I live in the middle. The Morning Glory is practically sabotage central."

He gave me that slow blink, the one that meant I was impossible and he'd already made his peace with it.

Sadie came bounding back with a construction-paper star clamped triumphantly in her teeth. One of the kids groaned. "Hey! She stole our decoration!"

I pried it from her jaws and returned it. "Sorry. She's got an overdeveloped sense of quality control."

The children laughed, and one crouched to scratch her ears. For a moment, tension eased.

Back at the inn, Hannah had turned the kitchen into an assembly line. Dozens of gingerbread men marched across the counters, some with lopsided scarves, others with icing buttons that looked suspiciously like freckles. Guests and locals alike pitched in, decorating with candy and sneaking bites when they thought Hannah wasn't looking.

"Don't eat the morale!" she scolded as Finn popped a cookie into his mouth.

"Quality control," he said, crumbs spraying.

In the parlor, Barb stationed herself at the window with binoculars borrowed from Doris, muttering about "suspicious mail carriers" and "the likelihood of reindeer espionage."

By dusk, the town square glowed again—not with electricity, but with hundreds of candles in glass jars. They lined the paths, circled the tree, and sat in every shop window. The effect was breathtaking: a golden sea of light pushing back the December dark.

The choir director, voice still trembling, led a handful of singers through *Silent Night*. The harmony wavered at first but steadied as neighbors joined, their voices rising into the crisp air.

I stood shoulder to shoulder with Matt, Sadie pressed against my boots. Around us, neighbors sang, laughed, and held one another close. For the first time in days, the knot in my chest loosened.

"This," Matt said softly, "is what they can't sabotage."

I looked up at him, at the tired lines etched by worry, at the determination still burning in his eyes. "We'll find them," I said.

"We will," he agreed. "But even if we don't tonight... the town wins anyway."

Barb appeared at my elbow, notebook clutched like a relic, eyes glistening in the candlelight. "I admit, this is beautiful. But don't let your guard down. The enemy thrives on complacency."

I smiled despite myself. "Barb, can't we just enjoy one song?"

She sniffed. "Fine. But only one."

The song swelled, candles flickered, and the air seemed to hold its breath. For all the sabotage, for all the fear, Marigold Lake hadn't folded. And standing there with Matt beside me, Sadie at my feet, and the town glowing with stubborn hope, I felt it too—something stronger than fear.

Christmas spirit, bruised but unbroken.

Chapter Sixteen

The Great Marigold Town Meeting

By the time I got to City Hall, I was already regretting volunteering to take notes. The place looked less like a council chamber and more like a snow globe that had been shaken too hard: people packed shoulder-to-shoulder in puffy coats, stamping snow from their boots, voices rising in overlapping chatter. The scent of cocoa and wet mittens mixed with drooping pine garland from the rafters, making the whole room smell like Christmas in a laundromat.

The space buzzed so intensely it felt like static was hanging in the air. Old ceiling fans rattled from the warm breath of so many bodies packed into one place, and every time the front doors opened a rush of cold spiraled in, sending a flurry of snowflakes drifting like tiny sparks above the crowd. Somewhere in the middle of it all, someone was arguing about whether city hall's thermostat was intentionally sabotaged as well. Typical.

Sadie trotted at my side, ears pricked, nub tail wagging like she was ready to take the minutes herself.

At least someone seemed confident. Every now and then, a mittened hand reached down to pat her head, and she accepted the attention like a seasoned politician shaking hands at a rally. Her presence alone seemed to steady a few nerves—proof that in Marigold Lake, even the town dog carried emotional-support responsibilities.

At the front, the mayor banged a wooden gavel. "Order, please!"

The sound barely carried over the hiss of winter boots and the scrape of metal chairs being dragged across the tile floor. The fluorescent lights above flickered as if overwhelmed by the sheer volume of exasperation in the room.

The sound was immediately swallowed by the Petersons, who were loudly arguing over whether their front-yard reindeer display was superior to their neighbor's.

"Order!" the mayor barked again.

Barb popped up like a jack-in-the-box, notebook in hand. "If you're looking for order, you're in the wrong town. But if you're looking for the truth—" She held her notebook aloft like a manifesto. "—I've got it right here."

A ripple went through the room—half hopeful, half horrified—because everyone knew Barb's notebook was equal parts chaos and conspiracy. A few people sank deeper into their seats, bracing for impact.

Mavis strode down the aisle with her scarf trailing like a battle banner. "Sit down, Barb. We haven't even heard the agenda yet."

"Agenda?" Barb sniffed. "The agenda is sabotage. The agenda is conspiracy. The agenda is saving Christmas!"

The mayor rubbed his temples. "For the record, the agenda is 'community updates,' followed by cocoa and cookies."

Sadie barked as if seconding the cocoa.

Hannah bustled in from the back, cheeks pink from balancing trays of gingerbread. "Everyone eat something and stop yelling before I start throwing cookies."

The trays she carried wobbled dangerously every time someone shouted, and I had a brief vision of gingerbread shrapnel flying across the chamber. Given Hannah's current stress level, it wasn't far-fetched.

That bought us about thirty seconds of calm.

Then Doris Temple climbed onto her chair, binoculars bouncing against her chest. "I saw them!" she cried. "Two figures in the square last night. One was tall, cloaked, moving fast. The other was... glowing. Probably alien."

Groans filled the chamber.

"Or maybe," Mavis said, "it was Pete hauling his garbage can."

"Pete doesn't glow!" Doris retorted.

Sadie barked sharply, casting her vote with Mavis.

Meanwhile, Finn had plugged his laptop into an outlet near the podium and was tapping furiously, wires spilling from his bag like ivy. "If everyone could stop screaming, I'm trying to cross-reference power surges with porch cam footage."

"Cross-reference this," Mr. Peterson shouted, waving a mittened fist. "My cocoa urn exploded last night—I nearly drowned in marshmallows!"

"Sabotage by sugar!" Barb scribbled furiously.

"No," Mrs. Peterson said tartly, "it was sabotage by your clumsiness."

"See?" Barb spun toward the crowd. "They can't even agree on marshmallows! We're under psychological attack."

Doris cupped her hands like a prophet. "I've been saying it for years—aliens use marshmallows to weaken our defenses. They're soft, they're sticky, they lull you into complacency."

Someone in the back muttered, "They lull me into hot cocoa."

The chamber erupted again, but despite the absurdity, I could feel the unease hiding beneath the jokes. People weren't just laughing—they were trying to laugh *instead* of panicking.

Sadie, apparently inspired, leapt onto a chair and snatched a gingerbread man straight from the tray. The room gasped. She sat proudly, icing stuck to her whiskers, every inch the canine deputy mayor.

The mayor sighed into his gavel. "Enough! We need one clear suspect. One. Who's got evidence?"

For the first time all night, the room hushed.

The silence was sharp, almost brittle, like everyone was holding the same breath. Even the radiator stopped clanking, as if waiting for the answer.

All eyes turned to Matt, standing tall at the back. Snow dusted his coat; his expression was steady as stone. He stepped forward, holding up a plastic bag with a frayed rope inside. The cut ends glinted under the fluorescent lights.

"This," Matt said, voice even but firm, "was found behind the bandstand. Sawed through. Clean. Deliberate."

A murmur swept through the chairs—fear, curiosity, accusation all blending together. Someone whispered a prayer. Someone else whispered, "I knew it," though I doubted they knew what "it" even was.

Gasps rippled. Someone dropped a cookie. Sadie darted forward, snapped it up, and sat back down as if she'd been deputized.

"And," Matt continued, "that rope was found in a box delivered to one person in this town. Oliver Trent."

The room erupted—half shouts, half whispers.

"Outsider!" Barb shrieked.

"Maple Valley plant!" Doris wailed.

"Probably an alien in disguise!" someone added.

"Not helping," Matt muttered.

I scanned the crowd, heart hammering. Grace Holloway clutched her box of unsold ornaments like prayer beads. The Petersons were arguing over whether Oliver had once borrowed a hammer at their garage sale and "forgot" to return it. Hannah pressed a cookie into Mavis's hand like it was ammunition.

And Oliver himself? He wasn't even there. Which, in Marigold Lake logic, was proof enough for half the town.

The mayor banged the gavel, but Barb had already climbed onto a chair, notebook raised like a battle flag. "Ladies and gentlemen," she declared, "Christmas has an enemy—and his name is Oliver Trent!"

Sadie barked so loud the windows rattled.

The room dissolved into pandemonium—neighbors shouting, chairs scraping, mitten strings tangling. Through it all, Matt stood steady, shoulders squared, expression grim.

The weight of the moment pressed in around me. The tension, the fear, the wild accusations swirling through the room like a blizzard—none of it was easing. If anything, the storm was picking up speed.

I exhaled, watching the madness swirl. For all the uproar, the finger-pointing, the alien accusations, one thing was clear: the saboteur wasn't finished.

And neither were we.

Chapter Seventeen

The Culprit Revealed

The town square felt different the next morning. Not calmer, exactly—more like the collective hangover after a disaster party. The Christmas tree had been braced upright, ornaments swept into boxes, cocoa stains half-scrubbed from the sidewalks. The air carried that bruised quiet of a community trying very hard not to panic.

The cold bit a little sharper than usual, as if even the weather was hesitant about what came next. A few stray glitter flecks—remnants of some child's ornament or Barb's stress crafting—caught the weak sunlight and glimmered in the snow. The benches held patches of frost where people had sat late into the night, whispering theories into steaming cups of cocoa. Even the lampposts seemed to lean inward, as though the square itself was listening, waiting, bracing.

Matt and I stood at the edge of the square with steaming travel mugs. Sadie perched like a sentinel on the bench between us, nub tail twitching every time a volunteer marched past with a ladder or a string of lights.

I could feel the tension rolling off the volunteers, the way they spoke in clipped sentences and nervous laughter. People kept glancing toward the tree as if afraid it might fall again despite the braces. Every hammer tap echoed like a warning bell. Sadie's ears flicked at every sound, alert, watchful, her little body wound tight like a spring.

"Half the town still thinks Maple Valley's behind it," I said, watching Barb sweep by with her notebook held like scripture.

Barb marched with the purpose of a military commander inspecting her troops. Every few steps she jotted something down, muttering phrases like *psychological warfare* and *cocoa-based clues*. A few townsfolk kept a safe distance, as if proximity might land them in the next chapter of her manifesto.

"They're not," Matt said grimly. He'd barely touched his coffee. "The cuts on the tree ropes were clean. Professional. Someone knew how to bring it down without killing anyone—just enough for a spectacle."

His voice held that tight edge he used when cases got under his skin. The kind that made him stay up late staring at files or drive the long way home just to think. He kept scanning the square, taking in every movement—the lights, the cords, the volunteers, the tree. The detective gears in his brain were spinning faster than the town's rumor mill.

"Festive sabotage with a side of public humiliation," I said. "That takes planning."

Sadie huffed her agreement. A passing child giggled and whispered, "The dog knows things," which, in Marigold Lake, was practically gospel.

"It also takes access," he said, following my gaze to the diner. Through its frosted windows, Oliver Trent sat in his usual booth. Notebook open. Pen moving. Scarf tied with the precision of a man about to attend a coronation.

The sight of him sent a ripple of unease through me. He always looked too composed, too tidy, even after the tree collapse. People reacting to chaos usually wore it on their sleeves—frazzled hair, crooked scarves, wild eyes. Not Oliver. He looked like he ironed his thoughts before sharing them.

Sadie growled, a tiny engine revving.

"Subtle, she's not," I murmured, scratching her ears.

Her gaze didn't leave the diner window. Dogs could sense storms before they happened. Maybe sabotage counted as one.

Matt set his mug on the bench. "Stay here."

"Oh, absolutely not. If you think I'm letting you corner Mr. Suspicious Notebook alone, you haven't been paying attention."

He gave me a look—half exasperation, half something softer. The kind of look that said he'd learned fighting me on this was pointless. He inhaled, resigned to my involvement the way one accepts Iowa winters.

His jaw ticked, but he didn't argue—which, from Matt, was basically a declaration of love.

The diner smelled like bacon and burnt coffee. Hannah and Finn were already there, pretending to split pancakes while actually spying on Oliver from two booths away. Hannah gave a quick wave; Finn adjusted the salt shaker like it was surveillance gear.

The bell over the door jingled behind us as more townspeople trickled in, hoping for warmth, gossip, or possibly a front-row seat if things got dramatic. A teenager dropped a muffin at the sight of Matt's badge. An older man scooted over without being asked, freeing the aisle like we were carrying a bomb instead of a dog.

Oliver looked up as we approached, that too-polite smile in place. He closed the notebook just a fraction too slowly. "Detective. Ms. Fisher. To what do I owe the pleasure?"

"Cut the pleasantries," Matt said, sliding into the seat across from him. I squeezed in beside Matt so Sadie could hop into my lap and glare across the table like a furry prosecuting attorney.

Sadie planted both paws on the table edge, one ear cocked forward in full interrogation posture. She was the only creature in town allowed to put her paws on diner furniture without getting scolded.

"Strong company you keep," Oliver murmured.

"Stronger evidence," Matt said. He set a clear plastic bag on the table: a frayed length of rope. The cut gleamed—clean, deliberate.

A hush fell around us as nearby diners leaned in. Even the fry cook paused mid-flip.

Oliver's eyes flicked down, then back. "And?"

"And I found it behind the bandstand," Matt said evenly. "Right next to a hardware-store box addressed to you."

That part was new. My eyebrows shot up.

Hannah almost dropped her fork. Finn mouthed *WHAT?* dramatically.

"I order supplies often," Oliver said smoothly. "For sketches. For... installations."

"Ropes and industrial glue?" Matt asked, voice like ice. "Funny art supplies."

Oliver's smile strained. I could practically hear the gears grinding as he recalculated his story.

I leaned in, Sadie squirming against my arm. "You've been circling words for days—lighting, carols, parade route, weak spots. That's not sketching, Oliver. That's planning."

For the first time, his smile faltered.

Finn materialized with the syrup bottle like a weapon. "Also, you left your trunk open last night. Boxes labeled Stage Equipment. Pretty sure that's not on the Marigold Lake shopping list."

A nearby table gasped. Someone muttered, "Knew it. Outsiders always go for stage equipment."

"Spying, were you?" Oliver asked, eyes sharpening.

"Investigating," Finn said cheerfully. "Like Scooby-Doo, but with fewer snacks."

"Speak for yourself," Hannah said, tugging the syrup away from him.

Hannah swiveled in the booth behind us, chin propped on her hands. "So what's the plan? Sabotage the tree, ruin the carols, humiliate the mayor—and then what? Sell a tell-all to Maple Valley? Launch a one-man Grinch tour?"

"You wouldn't understand," he said, smile cooling.

"Try me," I said.

Oliver's gaze skimmed the diner. Half the town had stopped pretending not to listen. Barb hovered by the pie case, pencil poised for her headline.

"I was hired," he said at last.

The words rippled through the room.

The cook swore under his breath. A baby hiccuped. Barb let out an audible gasp and almost slid off her stool.

"By who?" Matt asked.

"People who wanted your festival to fail," Oliver said. "Not Maple Valley as a whole—donors. The kind who benefit when Marigold Lake stops drawing tourists. Pay enough, and a rumor here, a failure there... people do the rest. Collapse the festival, shift the money. Maple Valley wins."

"That's insane," Hannah breathed.

"And yes," Oliver added, almost bored, "BahHumbug42 was me."

A susurrus of whispers rose. Barb fogged the pie case glass with a gasp. Sadie barked once—sharp—and launched herself onto the table before I could stop her. Her paws smacked the notebook; the cover flipped, pages splaying.

Sketches of the square. Notes in neat print: weak point—tree ropes; replace music sheets; sabotage extension cords.

The diner gasped in unison.

Several pancakes went cold as their owners forgot they were there. The mayor's cousin dropped his spoon. Someone whispered, "Knew it. Always the scarf wearers."

Matt swept up the notebook, scanning page after page. His jaw set. "That's enough."

Oliver tried to stand, but Finn blocked the aisle, syrup bottle ready. "Sit. Down."

The bell over the door jingled. Two uniformed officers stepped in—Matt must have called them earlier, just in case.

The officers took in the scene with matching expressions that said, *Yep, this tracks for Marigold Lake.*

"Mr. Trent," Matt said, rising smoothly, "you're under arrest for reckless endangerment, destruction of property, and sabotage of a public event."

Oliver's composure cracked, smile going brittle. "You don't understand. They'll just hire someone else. This isn't over."

"Maybe not," Matt said, handing the notebook to an officer, "but it's over for you."

They cuffed him. His scarf trailed like a deflated flag as the door shut behind them. The diner erupted into relieved chatter.

Grace Holloway lingered near the entrance, eyes wide. For a moment I thought she'd be next on Matt's list, but when she spoke her voice shook. "So it wasn't me."

"It wasn't you," Matt said, gentler now.

Relief washed over her. She slipped out quietly, clutching her ornament box like proof she belonged.

Two more threads tied off by evening. The missing Santa suit turned up at the community theater—checked out for a dress rehearsal and never logged back in, an honest mix-up with terrible timing. And Baby Jesus? Found in the First Methodist youth room with a cracked base and a note: meant to fix. No one owned up. It felt like its own small confession—careless hands at the worst moment, not sabotage.

Whispers spread quickly—of embarrassment, of apologies, of *thank goodness it wasn't worse.* The town, for once, let out a collective exhale. Even the air seemed warmer.

Back at the Morning Glory, the parlor hummed with cautious celebration. Guests sipped cocoa. Hannah brought out cinnamon rolls with extra frosting. Barb had already stapled a fresh sign to her notebook: CASE CLOSED.

Finn stood by the fire trying to explain Ohm's law to Mavis, who stared at him like he was reciting wizard spells. The Petersons clinked mismatched mugs in a toast. Doris claimed she predicted Oliver's downfall "from the moment he walked in wearing that coat."

"Do you think he was telling the truth?" I asked Matt quietly, watching firelight skate across his features.

"About being hired?" He nodded. "Probably. But whether it was Maple Valley donors or just his excuse for being greedy—that still needs proof."

"And you'll get it," I said.

Matt's eyes softened. Just a shade. The kind of softness he usually saved for after the danger passed.

He gave me a look—equal parts stern and warm. "Not if you keep sticking your nose in."

"You'd be bored without me."

Sadie hopped into my lap, nub tail thumping as if she agreed.

Around us, Finn attempted to fix Barb's antique lights (with predictable sparks), Hannah snuck an extra swirl of icing onto her own roll, and guests laughed for the first time in days.

Christmas in Marigold Lake wasn't saved yet. The star was still missing. The choir was still scattered. But the saboteur had been caught, the truth was out, and for tonight at least, hope glowed as bright as the tree soon would again.

I looked at Matt, at Sadie, at the cozy, chaotic family we'd built, and thought: maybe gingerbread couldn't fix everything. But it came awfully close.

Chapter Eighteen

Mistletoe and Mayhem

The Morning Glory smelled like cinnamon, pine, and victory.

For the first time in weeks, there was no whisper of sabotage, no nervous glances toward the square. The saboteur was gone, the lights were steady, and Marigold Lake was ready to celebrate.

Yet even with the calm settling over town, a faint haze of disbelief lingered in the air—like everyone expected another shoe to drop or a rogue string of lights to explode. People kept pausing at windows, checking the street, confirming that yes, Christmas was allowed to breathe again. Even I found myself glancing at the porch cameras as I passed by, habit refusing to let go just yet.

The parlor gleamed like a magazine spread—if the magazine was *Chaotic Holiday Living.* Tinsel draped across every surface, wreaths framed the windows, and a fire roared in the hearth. Guests gathered with cocoa and Hannah's cookies, their laughter mingling with carols from Finn's begrudging Bluetooth speaker.

Every seat was full. Every mug steamed. Even the ancient radiator seemed to hum merrily instead of wheeze its usual death rattle. Someone had strung popcorn garland along the banister again, though it was unclear whether this was festive decor or a desperate attempt to keep Sadie from eating it off the lower branches.

Barb had draped herself across the sofa like a queen awaiting coronation, her blinking BELIEVE sweater nearly outshining the tree. "I knew it all along," she announced for the fiftieth time. "My notes were crucial to the arrest."

A couple of guests exchanged amused glances, and one whispered, "I think her sweater is brighter than the emergency lights during the blackout." Barb either didn't hear or pretended she hadn't, choosing instead to adjust her blinking collar as if preparing for a photoshoot.

Finn groaned from behind his laptop, half-watching cat videos, half-resetting the speaker. "Yeah, nothing says airtight case like 'sticky fingers equals guilt.'"

From somewhere in the corner, someone snorted into their cocoa. Finn kept tapping away at the speaker settings, muttering about firmware updates and how polka remixes shouldn't be allowed near Christmas carols.

Barb bristled. "That was a pivotal observation."

Behind her, Mavis arched a brow so high it nearly hit her reindeer headband. But she said nothing—probably saving her commentary for a more dramatic moment.

"Pretty sure it was Sadie," Finn countered, glancing toward the Boston Terrier snoozing happily by the hearth. "She's the real hero."

Sadie lifted her head at her name, gave a satisfied huff, and went back to dreaming of gingerbread.

Even her snores sounded smug, like she was well aware her contribution had outweighed at least half the human effort in town. Someone placed a small fleece blanket over her back, and Sadie immediately curled tighter into it, blissfully content.

"History will vindicate me," Barb said loftily, scribbling *Heroine* in large looping letters across her notepad.

She underlined it twice, then drew what appeared to be an overly muscular stick figure version of herself wielding a magnifying glass like a sword. It was... something.

"History's going to roll its eyes," Hannah muttered as she swept in with a tray of gingerbread men. Her apron was dusted with flour, her cheeks pink from the heat. "Eat these before I have to frost another batch. And don't touch the tin marked *Do Not Tamper*. That's for quality control."

One of the B&B guests—an older gentleman with jingle bells attached to his suspenders—leaned toward the cookies with reverence. "These look like the kind of pastries people write songs about."

"Eat them," Hannah said. "Don't serenade them."

"Who's controlling the quality?" Finn asked, already reaching.

"Me." Hannah smacked his hand with a spatula.

The crack echoed across the room like a mini thunderclap. Hannah handed the tray to a nearby family, who accepted it as though it contained sacred relics.

The Petersons bickered over who got the cookie with the most gumdrops, while the Millers traded stories of Christmases spent on the road. Mavis directed ornament placement like a general: "Higher. No, higher. Lift with your knees, not your back." Poor Dennis the volunteer looked like he'd enlisted in holiday boot camp.

Dennis wobbled on a step stool, holding a glittery ornament in one trembling hand while Mavis gestured wildly at the tree. "You're tilting! Don't tilt! The ornament is a metaphor for life—BALANCED!"

For once, nobody minded. The sabotage was behind us. The town had rallied. Tonight, the Morning Glory wasn't just a bed-and-breakfast—it was the beating heart of Marigold Lake.

A faint hum of relief thrummed through the walls, like the building itself was inhaling for the first time since December began. Lanterns flickered in the windows. Snow drifted outside in calm little spirals. The whole place looked like a postcard labeled *Finally, Some Peace.*

I stood in the middle of it all, arms folded, smiling until my cheeks ached. This was Christmas: messy, loud, full of crumbs and carols.

And for the first time, the mess felt good—not like a symptom of incoming disaster, but a reminder of how deeply this town loved being together, even when its decorations were crooked and its nerves had been fried.

The side door opened, letting in a swirl of snow. Matt stepped inside, stamping his boots, coat dusted white. His eyes swept the room, then landed on me. Something in his shoulders eased, like he'd been carrying the town's weight and could finally set it down.

He looked softer tonight—shadows gone from under his eyes, posture looser. Even the lingering detective tension had melted from his jaw, replaced by the weariness of a man who finally had a moment to breathe.

"Detective Hale!" Barb cried, springing to her feet. "Come here. You must be properly thanked by the citizens you serve."

He gave her a look that could've curdled eggnog. "I'm just here for coffee."

Someone in the back murmured, "Sure you are," earning a few snickers.

"Coffee and gratitude," Barb corrected.

Matt muttered something that sounded suspiciously like "God help me," but before he could argue, Hannah thrust a mug into his hand. "Drink. You've earned it."

He shot me a wry smile over the rim, and my heart did that ridiculous flutter it always seemed to do around him.

There was something so comforting about the way he held a mug—steady, solid, like even the cocoa knew it was safe with him. It hit me again just how much calmer the room felt when he was in it.

Then Barb gasped, pointing toward the archway. "Mistletoe!"

I froze.

My brain scrambled through the possibilities—is this a trap? A decoration I hadn't approved? Another one of Barb's schemes?—but no, it was unmistakable.

Sure enough, a sprig hung from the doorway, tied with a red ribbon. Fresh. Suspiciously fresh.

"Oh, for—" I began.

"Mistletoe law!" Barb declared. "Page twelve of the holiday bylaws. Look it up."

"There are no holiday bylaws," Matt said, though his tone lacked conviction.

Someone whispered, "There SHOULD be," and the room nodded in collective agreement.

The room went silent, every guest suddenly very interested in the scene. The Petersons leaned forward. The Millers whispered. Even Mavis allowed herself the faintest smile.

The quiet was charged, expectant. Even the fire crackled softer, as though giving us space for the moment to land.

Sadie—traitor that she was—sat neatly at my feet, nub tail thumping like a drumroll.

Matt sighed, the sound of a man surrendering to fate. He stepped closer, his eyes warm despite the exasperation etched in his face. "Better get this over with," he murmured.

Before I could overthink it, he kissed me. Soft. Warm. Steady.

It wasn't dramatic. It wasn't showy. It was calm and sure and felt like stepping into a room lit by candlelight—the kind of kiss that said: finally.

The parlor erupted.

Barb fanned herself with her notebook. Hannah whooped. Finn whistled.

Someone shouted, "ABOUT TIME!" which was rude but not inaccurate.

"Finally," Mavis muttered, though her lips twitched in amusement.

I pulled back, laughing, breathless. Matt gave me a look equal parts fond and exasperated.

"Happy now?" he asked Barb.

"Ecstatic," she said. "Consider Christmas saved."

Sadie barked, then leapt into Matt's lap, smearing his coat with gingerbread crumbs. He scratched her ears and muttered, "You're easier than your owner."

"Hey!" I protested, though I couldn't stop smiling.

Sadie puffed her chest with obvious pride, as though she believed she had personally orchestrated the entire moment.

The rest of the evening blurred in a haze of food, laughter, and the comforting chaos of friends who had become family. Guests exchanged small gifts, Hannah produced yet another tray of cookies, Finn coaxed the speaker into behaving for a grand total of six minutes before it switched back to polka carols, and Barb insisted on a dramatic reading from "the case of the century."

At one point, Dennis tried to hang another ornament under Mavis's supervision and nearly toppled the tree. Someone started an impromptu carol that turned into a three-part harmony. The Petersons declared a temporary cease-fire of their cookie war. And the Millers promised to come back next year "unless Marigold Lake bans polka."

Through it all, the tree glowed steady and strong. Still missing its proper star, patched with paper ornaments and borrowed strands of lights, but shining all the same.

Its mismatched bulbs flickered in warm oranges and reds, giving the whole parlor a soft, nostalgic glow. It looked like something stitched together by love and stubbornness—exactly what it was.

For the first time in weeks, I wasn't thinking about sabotage or suspects. Just Christmas. Just here. Just us.

And Sadie, curled between me and Matt, snoring into the warmth of the blankets, seemed to agree.

Epilogue

Later that evening, after the last cocoa mug was washed and the last guest tucked into bed, I slipped out to the porch with Sadie trotting at my heels. The air was crisp, the kind that bit at your nose but left the sky so clear you could see every star the saboteur hadn't managed to steal.

The porch boards creaked under my boots as I stepped out, each groan of the wood familiar and oddly comforting—like the house exhaling after the longest week of its life. Warm light spilled from the windows behind me, soft and golden, framing the parlor full of discarded cookie crumbs and half-finished mugs. The chaos had finally settled, leaving behind that quiet hum of contentment that only comes after a town chooses hope over panic.

I wrapped my coat tighter and sank into the old rocking chair. Sadie leapt into my lap, a warm little weight against the cold. She gave a sigh that sounded suspiciously like satisfaction.

For a moment, I listened to the small sounds—the distant crunch of someone shoveling, the faint jingle of a wreath in the wind, the soft hiss of snow drifting off the railing. Christmas Eve-eve, the locals called it. A time for breathing before the real celebration kicked in. I hadn't realized how much I needed that breath until tonight.

The porch creaked, and a familiar shadow filled the doorway. Matt stepped out, shoulders broad in his peacoat, hair dusted with snowflakes. He carried two steaming mugs and handed one to me without a word.

"Thanks," I said softly.

He sat beside me, the rocking chair groaning under his weight. For a while we just sipped in companionable silence, watching the Christmas lights flicker weakly along the eaves.

I glanced at him from the corner of my eye. The tension he'd been wearing like armor all week had eased—just enough that I could see the man beneath the badge again. The one who remembered to bring me cocoa even when he forgot to eat dinner. The one who always made space beside him without asking if I would take it.

"Crazy day," I finally said.

"Understatement," he replied dryly. "Tree sabotage, near-riot, mistletoe ambush..." His mouth curved. "Not the kind of report I usually file."

I smiled into my mug. "You survived."

"Barely." He glanced at me, eyes softer now. "But it was... worth it."

Heat curled low in my chest that had nothing to do with the cocoa. Sadie, apparently sensing the moment, hopped down to the floorboards and curled up at our feet, giving a pointed yawn.

The quiet between us stretched, full but gentle—like the hush right before the first carol begins. Snow dusted the railings in delicate layers, and the world felt wrapped in its own soft blanket.

Finally, Matt leaned closer, voice low. "Promise me something, Claire."

"What's that?"

"When this all shakes out—whoever's behind it—you'll let me handle the dangerous part."

I wanted to say yes. I wanted to promise I'd stay on the porch, safe with Sadie, while he solved everything like a proper detective. But I couldn't. Not when I knew myself. Not when I knew this town.

"I'll promise to notice," I said instead.

He gave me that long, steady look, the one that said he saw straight through me. Then he sighed, shaking his head with a rueful smile.

"Figured that's the best I'd get."

His hand brushed mine briefly—a touch so small I might've imagined it if my heart hadn't stuttered in my chest. For a second neither of us moved, both pretending the moment wasn't as charged as it felt.

We rocked in silence again, the snow falling soft around us, the lights glowing faintly above. And for that quiet moment—despite saboteurs, chaos, and mystery—I felt like Christmas had given us exactly what we needed.

Together. On the porch. Watching the stars no one could steal.

And there on that quiet porch, wrapped in snow and starlight, I knew we were ending the season exactly the way Christmas should end—together, warm, safe, and ready for whatever came next.

Coming Soon

Coming Soon: The Valentine's Vendetta at the Morning Glory

Love is in the air at Marigold Lake... until sabotage crashes the Sweetheart Social.

Claire Fisher has her hands full with a packed B&B, a town-wide Valentine's dance, and Hannah's high-stakes dessert contest. But when stolen love letters, a spiked chocolate fountain, and a missing heirloom locket turn romance into chaos, it's clear someone is nursing more than a broken heart.

With Detective Matt Hale trying to keep the peace, Barb launching her "love investigation service," and Sadie the Boston Terrier playing accidental matchmaker, Claire will have to untangle a web of jealousies, rivalries, and secret admirers before the town's sweetest celebration turns sour.

Can love—and Marigold Lake—survive a Valentine's vendetta?

About the author

Reva Davenport writes cozy mysteries filled with small-town charm, holiday spirit, and just enough mischief to keep you turning the pages. She is the author of *A Marigold Lake Cozy Mystery* series, where Claire Fisher, her Boston Terrier Sadie, and the colorful townsfolk of Marigold Lake stumble into secrets, sabotage, and sleuthing between cups of cocoa.

When she's not writing, Reva loves boutique treasure-hunting, fresh-baked cookies, and small-town celebrations that feel like they belong in a snow globe. She believes every mystery is better with laughter, a loyal pup at your side, and a touch of holiday magic.

Stay connected with Reva Davenport:

Visit: revadavenport.com

Join her newsletter for updates, sneak peeks, and exclusive bonuses

Follow along on Facebook & Instagram for cozy updates (and plenty of Sadie cameos!)

Also by Reva Davenport

<u>A Marigold Lake Cozy Mystery Series</u>
Secrets Buried in the Backyard
Dead Air at the Morning Glory
The Suitcase at the Morning Glory
Flour Power at the Morning Glory
The Missing Brooch at the Morning Glory
My Sister at the Morning Glory
Christmas at the Morning Glory